Excitable Women, Damaged Men

Robert Boyers

Excitable

Women, Damaged Men

Turtle Point Press New York 2005

Copyright © 2005 by Turtle Point Press

LCCN 2001012345 ISBN 1-885586-40-x

Design and composition by Jeff Clark
at Wilsted & Taylor Publishing Services

The author would like to express his gratitude
to the editors of the following periodicals,
in which these stories originally appeared:
Harvard Review, "An Excitable Woman";
The Ontario Review, "Samantha"
(Cooper Prize Story); *New Letters*,
"A Perfect Stranger"; *Parnassus*,
"The Visit"; *Southwest Review*, "Torso"
and "Tribunal"; *Michigan Quarterly Review*,
"In Hiding"; *Notre Dame Review*, "The French
Lesson"; *Yale Review*, "Secrets and Sons."

To Peg Boyers and Barbara Moore

Excitable Women, Damaged Men

An Excitable Woman

Twice she screamed. Twice only. When we found her—it couldn't have taken us more than a few seconds—she had her face pressed against the rough surface of the suspended carpet, arms extended, the body taut, erect, expectant. Come out of there, mom, I said. Just move out slowly, towards me. At which she turned her face ever so slightly in my direction, a look of mild panic on her features, until, in seconds, a slow smile broke across her mouth and she said, softly, I'm losing my mind.

She was more or less healthy then, and she hadn't quite lost her mind. She was, as she often said, nervous, excitable, occasionally hysterical. But she knew what was what. That too she often asserted. She knew what was what. She knew that, at the vast lower Fifth Avenue emporium, we were hoping to buy an oriental rug with money we didn't have. She knew that this was not unusual for us, this deliberate extravagance, and that afterwards we'd have no regrets. She knew that we tried to include her in our activities, and that she was rarely grateful. Trying to prove something, she would say. That you like my company. That you like me. And she knew that in part this was the truth, though also ungenerous and not an endearing expression of our efforts to get along with one another.

It was a sprawling place we'd taken her to, with several floors of carpets, most of them layered by size in three- or four-foot-high stacks, a number of choice items hung from ceiling racks, so that it was possible to walk between them, occasionally to push one back to examine it without having to press your face up against it. Rose wouldn't have known how to distinguish a Killim from a Kerastan. Though she couldn't tell us what she was doing pressing herself between the enormous Indian rugs with the tree of life patterns in deep reds and greens, we figured she'd moved deliberately in there to escape our incessant chatter. Anything, even suffocation, was preferable to another exchange on the merits of Iranian or Kurdish design. If you asked her, you could save a lot of money and headache by ordering a nice wall to wall carpet from the outlet store in her neighborhood. Professors, she said, have a thing about "oriental." They think it's classy. But they don't give a damn when someone trips on a fringe or the rug slides out of place.

She'd erupted more than a few times in those years. Nervous, she said. Suddenly afraid of things. Not wanting to find herself, suddenly, alone. Didn't like the darkness, the coming on of night, even in the house, with the lights on, the television blaring, the curtains or venetian blinds drawn tight against the menace, whatever it was or might have been. She screamed, she told us, several times she had cried out against the unnamed terrors, though she hadn't much gone in before for screaming, preferred a quieter though no less ostentatious desperation. And when she cried out, she said, it didn't much concern her that no one was around to hear or to cup a hand over her mouth. As long as she could tell us, so we would know what she was going through. Though of course no one gave a damn.

With the carpets, she said, she thought she'd never get out. The rough wool surface hurt her cheek. It felt to her like an assault, she could almost swear the thing actively slapped against her face, as if someone unseen just on the other side had made it slap against her. And then suddenly she felt herself about to faint, she wanted to reach for something, but there was nothing to hold on to, she was sure she would just collapse there and crumple up under the rugs where she'd stop breathing and no one would find her. I've lost so much weight, she said, that no one would see me or find me. They'd go on looking at the rugs and wouldn't notice me at all lying there in a neat little pile.

It surprised me that she slid out so compliantly when I called to her that day, though with her you had no reason to be surprised at anything. When, a few years earlier, my father left her for a much younger woman, she said she'd kill herself if he didn't come back — "I give him six months, that's all, and then I go up to the tallest building in the neighborhood, where he lives with that whore of his, and I time the jump to hit his wind-shield when he drives one morning out of the parking lot." But he didn't come back, and she didn't jump. Instead, she took driving lessons, at sixty, and for the first time bought herself a car. She joined a bridge club, took a trip to Atlantic City and wore red tortoise-shell sunglasses. She said, again and again, that her life wasn't worth living, that everything she touched turned to shit, but she got up each morning to go to work at the insurance company offices on East 23rd Street, and she complained bit-terly that her big-shot professor son and his big-shot poet-wife had failed to deliver her even one single grandchild. What are you waiting for? she asked. Till you can see the dirt in my mouth and the worms crawling out from between my toes?

Of course I was shocked the first time I got a call from someone at her office, who said I'd better get over there. Did something happen? I asked. Did she fall, or hit her head? No, she didn't fall, I was told. She's lying here on the floor, next to her desk, but she says nothing's the matter, and no, she won't talk to you on the phone. She wants to be left alone.

When I got there an hour or so later, I found her lying there still, her hands clasped comfortably under her head, staring intently up at the ceil-ing, the framed photograph of my dad squatting on her cluttered desk, her favorite piece of advice — "Be Glad You're Neurotic" — displayed on a bumper-sticker stuck to the window frame. Several of her colleagues greeted me as I moved up the crowded aisle, said they were glad to see me, and embarrassed. It's your son, Rose, one of them said as I stood at her feet. It's David. But she didn't shift her gaze from the ceiling, made no move to acknowledge me, so that I said, softly, firmly, nudging the sole of her stockinged foot with the toe of my shoe, get up, Rose, just get up from there right now. I didn't bend over her, didn't offer her a hand or kneel to show concern. I tried to maintain a steely demeanor, to communicate something short of anger, but not by much. And she responded to that, said, simply, get out of the way, then, just get out of the way, as she rolled over on her side and stood up, smiling graciously to the others who would, she knew, have a nice tidbit to share with their families that night. I reached then to brush off her clothes, but she swatted my hand away, shot me a look of offended majesty and, as if the others did not exist, asked what took me so long; she'd been waiting for me half the afternoon, was I busy? she asked, holding, emphasizing each of the syllables of the word, bu-sy?, reading a book maybe?, couldn't be disturbed?, not if your mother was lying on the floor and, for all you knew, might have hit her head on the edge of the desk or maybe swallowed a bottle of pills?

She was loathsome then, loathsome certainly to me, though I knew well enough that she was, fair enough, disturbed, not in perfect control. Her snow white, wrinkled skin and dyed black hair seemed to me then ghastly, and I wanted her just to be quiet, to accept that she'd done enough for one single day and to remain for once decently silent. I steered her gently by the elbow towards the comptroller's office at the end of the corridor and tried not to betray anything when she assured him she'd be alright the next day and back at her post. I couldn't tell what the man was thinking when he shook her hand and told her not to worry, that he'd see her tomorrow. Nor did her face register anything at all just then, as she turned and walked smartly to the elevator.

In the car a few minutes later she sat next to me, putting on some lipstick and checking her eyeliner in the rear-view mirror. Thanks for getting me, she said. I wanted to see how long it would take you. The words were uttered dryly, as if no sarcasm or criticism were intended. She did not turn her head to check my response. Neither did she turn towards me when I said she'd better not pull that sort of stunt again if she hoped to keep her job. To say nothing of the embarrassment, I added. I mean, won't you be sort of embarrassed when you go back tomorrow and face those people? Sure they like you—I gave that to her—but they'll have to wonder what's going on, if you aren't a real nutcase, won't they?

It's no big deal, she said, her hands demurely clasped on her lap, still staring straight ahead and now running a small brush through her thinning hair. They all think I'm eccentric anyway. You sure you don't mean crazy? I asked. So it's crazy, she said. What do I care what they think? A professor is looking over his shoulder. All the time he worries what someone will think of him. Me, I can lie on the floor and have the luxury not to care what they think.

It was no use, I concluded, doing my best to smile at her, my hands tight on the steering wheel, no use asking what she thought my part was in the drama she was, apparently, determined to play out. Did it matter to her that I hated to be brought in to her office and subjected to the pitying scrutiny of her colleagues? Obviously it did not occur to her that I was embarrassed. Or perhaps it did occur to her and she thought, good, let him know what it feels like to be humiliated, to have something happen to you that you can't control. High and mighty professors can use small doses of humiliation now and then. So she might well have told herself.

My mother had never been what you'd call a nice person. Candor was to her a primary virtue, and she was rarely comforting or solicitous even when, as a child, I was clearly hurting and in need of something beyond the assurance that I would get over this disappointment or that defeat. For an essentially modest woman she was a specialist in annihilating truths and withering sarcasms. A witness, now and then, to my father's gift for fellowship, his urgent wish to transmit to others some token of his fellow-feeling, a comradely arm flung over a shoulder, an innocent smile of endearment, she would ask him what exactly he was trying to prove, and to whom, and for what. It amused her to put him on the spot in that way, and she took an unmistakable satisfaction in noting his refusal to look any deeper than was his custom.

When at last he left her, after thirty years of marriage, it came as a shock only to those who did not really know them. He informed me of his irrevocable decision on a drive to Yankee Stadium one early September Sunday, and though I could hear in his voice apology, there was no trace in it of regret, and I had no heart to tell him I disapproved or would need time to take it in. Would I help him, he asked, to break it to Rose? That I would not, I said. Definitely not. My being there wouldn't help at all, I said, and worse, she'd know that we'd colluded somehow, as if I'd agreed to help you out against her. That's the way she's bound to see it, I said. If I help you I'm against her. And I don't want to be against her.

But of course we all knew that I was, precisely, against her. I'd never forgiven her for the small shocks and humiliations to which she'd subjected me through all the years of my growing up. If she was, as her own father used to say, a little crazy, it had always seemed to me that there was, in her craziness, a good deal of self-indulgence. Crazy people, I felt, allowed themselves to be crazy. When, in a fit of pique, she would throw a dinner plate against the kitchen wall, or dump a drawer full of silverware on the floor, I thought, even at eight or ten, shameful, disgusting. And when she warned me, her hand on my head, fingers fiercely wound through my pompadour, that something awful would happen if I so much as breathed a word about the dinner plate or silverware to my father, I thought, certainly by the age of twelve, bitch, and I hated her sugary, forced smiles when, a half hour later, my father came home from work, and I had to pretend that all was well.

Never, in those years, never in the adult years to come, did I try to put my arms around my mother and simply forgive her. More than once I recommended that she see a therapist, but she would laugh, her eyes would flash a kind of merry, insolent defiance, and she would point out to me that it was my own pride and fear of exposure that I was concerned about. Always, she would say, Mr. Big-shot is worried that his mother will make a scene and someone will think maybe he too is a little crazy.

My wife was better than I was with Rose, less reluctant to demonstrate unguarded commiseration. Often when we were together and Rose erupted, Phyllis would take her hand, stroke her arm, even occasionally kiss her sallow cheek. She would sit close to her at the dining room table in Rose's apartment, lean forward attentively, so that their faces might almost have touched, their breaths mingled. You hold yourself back, Phyllis would say to me when we were out of there at last, after what always seemed to me an interminable weekend afternoon. You seem so guarded, so off-center when you're around her.

But such things she said to me only in the first year or two of our marriage, before Rose had revealed herself to my darling wife, howled hysterically for her, uttered a few choice obscenities, intimated that she thought still about hiring someone to do something about my father and that woman of his. Quickly then Phyllis understood that I had reason to be careful with Rose, to protect myself from her furies and threats, from the unbearable intensity of her seizures and foreclosures. Was I afraid of my mother? I was, perpetually, afraid, dreaded her touch, her falsely ingratiating overtures, the sound of her voice on the telephone. I knew her, I felt, all too well, and suspected that she knew me to be, at bottom, weak, aversive, faithless.

When, three years after my father left her, she introduced us to a boyfriend, we made every effort to be welcoming. A retired bookkeeper, he was older than Rose by eight years, but seemed in much better shape. On their first visit to our place, Sam invited me to touch his bicep and soon showed me the pistol he carried in a holster neatly concealed beneath his brightly checkered jacket. He had a permit, he assured me, shot twice a week at a nearby gun club and worked out mornings at a fitness center. When he asked me to touch his stomach — hard as a rock — I declined and almost thanked the man for not pulling up his shirt to show it to me there in the brightly lit living room.

So you like him? Rose asked a day later. He's good looking, no? For a man that age?

He's presentable, Phyllis replied. Maybe a little bit, you know, over-enthusiastic.

So you didn't like him, Rose said. Too youthful, maybe. Too muscular, too too . . .

Why don't you ask David? Phyllis suggested. I can pass the phone to him.

Who needs David? Rose asked, when I can hear from you. Anyways, he won't have an opinion different from yours, and he won't tell me anything impolite. He's a good boy, my David, but he doesn't have a stomach for telling the truth. I trust you more than I trust him. And besides, I heard him pick up the receiver, and even if he holds his breath I can tell he's listening from the other room.

On our second afternoon with Sam he seemed impatient with my mother, intolerant of the food she served. He was, frankly, coarse and unpleasant, and when he spoke of the daughter he hadn't seen in years he complained that all she and her mother had ever wanted was to suck him dry. Looking hard at him and observing his tongue sweeping traces of brisket from between his teeth, I thought this the last man my mother needed to console herself.

But, as in so many things, I judged too quickly what my mother wanted. In almost every way, Sam was an ideal companion. He was, after all, a man to whom my mother might point with conviction and say, see what my life has become? You may once have thought there was hope for me, thought I deserved some compensation for my suffering and my years of loneliness. But no, that was never to be, as I knew, in spite of the soothing lies told me by my incorrigibly well-meaning son and his in every way impeccable wife.

Not that Rose ever said any such thing. She had no reason to explain anything, after all. She had only to sit quietly and watch me struggle to contain my exasperation when Sam regaled us with ugly little anecdotes or recounted the last time he shoved and threatened a much younger man who'd accidentally brushed against him at the pharmacy. No, there was no need for her to say a thing. She had only to watch the sordid little spectacle unfold and, with an expression mingling satisfaction and misery, hold out both her hands in utter defenseless resignation, as if to say, perfect, is he not?, so entirely the embodiment of a certain kind of nonentity to which the fates have inexorably consigned me?

Of course I tried to tolerate the man, tried not to despise him more than was absolutely necessary, for Rose's sake, obviously, and Phyllis tried no less. But it was hard, and it became harder when he moved in with her, and answered the phone whenever I called, and would not give way, not even when I said my time was limited and that I simply had to discuss something with my mother. Our monthly visits soon became hateful to us, Rose mostly silent, smiling, observant, Sam taking the lead in all things, rattling on, waving his hands about in a parody of animation, a swarm of nasal syllables assailing our ears, so that I thought more than once of commanding him to shut up, and speculated that he might then take hold of my narrow shoulders and toss me down the stairs.

But in fact we never quite came to the point of open hostility. I nursed my grievances in silence, and Phyllis contrived now and then to have others present when Rose and Sam came to us for lunch or dinner or a drive into the Catskills. Once, when Sam said something insulting to Phyllis about her poems—it's no wonder they don't pay you anything for such a book, there's hardly anything in it—I told him to be careful, not to talk about things he knew nothing about, and he replied that he had a right to say whatever he wanted to say, so that I ended the conversation by replying, just as simply, and without even raising my voice, that as we were in my car, I also had a right to pull over to the side of the road and put him out. No one said a word after that, or not until we got to the country inn in Ellenville where I'd made a dinner reservation, and Sam abusively berated the waitress for placing only two rolls in the bread basket and failing to refill his water glass. I merely looked on, unable to intercede on behalf of the waitress or to lure my mother from what had become her usual withdrawn, withholding silence. Here I sit, she seemed always to be saying, having brought you this magnificent emblem of my loss and futility, reconciled perfectly, as you see, with my circumstances and my fate.

But fate had other plans for Sam. A few days after our miserable Catskills excursion he was taken to Booth Memorial Hospital in Queens, where he died of congestive heart failure. He had made arrangements to be cremated, and my mother had no wish to convene a memorial service. Who would come? she asked. Not you, not Phyllis, not any of my bridge partners, who couldn't stand him and barely said hello to him when I had them over once or twice last year. So I phoned the lawyer he told me to call, and his daughter, and that's the end of it. Now I can eat by myself again, and look at a movie whenever I feel like it. And your father, he can think to himself, what will that woman put herself through next? All very nice, very tidy. You'll understand better as you go when I say that life is shit and the rest is make-believe. Trust me on this.

We laughed, Phyllis and I, about my mother's corrosive self-pity and her disparagement of all things finer and nicer than she felt herself to be. We marveled at the sharp, nasty turns of phrase she uttered and the inexorable darkness of her mind. She was, we often said, an original, one of a kind, distasteful, to be sure, but a person of a stubborn singleness of purpose, who felt that she had been put on earth to bear witness to the invincible rightness of her conviction that life is shit. It was hard not to accord to such a person some modicum of respect, and though Phyllis often wondered at my lack of affection for a woman who had been, after all, a devoted mother, she supposed that Rose would always have preferred respect to mere conventional affection, even from her son.

What bothered me occasionally was the thought, carefully planted and tended by my wife, that for all my protestations of disaffection, I enjoyed in my mother's company a sensation of power I allowed myself to experience with no one else. Yes, she did thwart, repel, unsettle me. She did, surely, inspire in me, as I so often said, genuine fear, if principally the fear of humiliation or exposure. But I knew myself to be, in a way that was unmistakable, central to her project of self-definition. Her refusal of any seemly accommodation or consolation was maintained principally on my behalf. It was not her colleagues she cared about when she acted out at the office: it was my discomfort she invited and savored. I was the object of her demonstrations; my wife, an oddly willing accomplice, was likewise a worthy witness to her defiant, sardonic miserableness. I had no power to call her out of her misery, but I exercised over her a sovereign power as the only person able to confer upon her existence some meaning, if only by virtue of my steady distaste for her and her principled unloveliness.

When I withdrew from her a year or so after Sam's death, I knew more or less what I was doing. Phyllis had given birth to our first child, a girl named Ella, and Rose had refused either to hold the child or to celebrate its coming into the world. Though she had wanted a grandchild, it now seemed to her, this new life, an affront, and she would not allow herself to weaken, not for a moment, not when she had been for so long resolute. She arrived one day at our door with a set of gifts: an infant playsuit, a mobile for hanging over the crib, a music box. She had put on a handsome herringbone tweed suit for the visit, and patent leather shoes with a bright silver buckle. But she barely looked at our new daughter, said she had been nursing a mild head cold and thought it best not to come too near to any of us. And that became the pattern of her subsequent, infrequent visits, even as our phone conversations then consisted of my mostly indifferent meander and her studied silence.

The result was that I phoned her less and less, and finally all but stopped inviting her over. If she wanted more from me, I felt, she could let me know, and if that seemed too hard, then the hell with her. I invited her, reluctantly, to join us for Thanksgiving dinner with Phyllis's parents, but she declined, tersely, said she was through with feast days and that we'd have a better time without her. No doubt she took some small satisfaction in my failure to contradict her on that last point at least.

Of course I wondered how she behaved at her bridge club and at work. Did she permit herself any enjoyment at all? Was there, perhaps, another man in her life? Had there been, I was sure, she would not have mentioned him to us on the rare occasions when we exchanged a few words, as we did some days before Christmas, when I suggested we pick her up and drive to a good restaurant in Port Washington for dinner overlooking the bay. She was busy, she said, spoken for. Is that so? I said. And where will you be going? Going nowhere, she said. But wouldn't you like to see Ella? I'll see her when we can have a conversation, she said. That will be soon enough, you know, when she can appreciate my scintillating wit. How do you know she can't appreciate you now? I asked. She can't be that precocious, Rose shot back. Not with you for a father. I'm not so slow, I said. You always did have a high opinion of yourself, she answered.

After that we didn't talk for more than three months. Phyllis phoned her several times and left messages expressing our desire to see her and to share Ella with her. But Rose never called back, and I figured that was that, and good riddance. Then Phyllis said she was worried, thought something was up, and decided to make what she called discreet inquiries. One Saturday she drove to Rose's bridge club, expecting to find her there, only to learn that she no longer played there on Saturday afternoons. On the following Monday she called Rose's office, asking to speak to her, and learned that Rose had retired a month or so earlier. You didn't know? the secretary asked.

That evening we bundled Ella into the car and drove to Rose's place, a first floor garden apartment in a Jewish neighborhood of Bayside. Identical red brick attached houses with carefully manicured lawns, broad sidewalks, grey benches out near the curb, numbered parking spaces, Rose's Plymouth Fury sheltered by the branches of a large, leafless maple. Standing by the benches, three elderly women in running shoes and silver warm-up jackets.

You want Rose? one woman almost shouted as we approached the cement stairs of my mother's unit. I didn't see her out all week, and she doesn't call me.

She doesn't call me either, I said.

Help me up with the carriage, Phyllis called, waiting at the foot of the stairs.

On the landing we settled the carriage and rang the bell, first briefly, then persistently, three times, four times. I could see through the half-open living room curtains that the tall halogen lamp beside the couch was burning brightly, and when I put my ear to the door I could hear the faint sound of the television in the tiny den that was at one time my bedroom. I rang again, and again, with no result, then leaned over the railing and managed to strike the bedroom window several times with my fist. Mom, I called, then louder, Rose? Mom?, we're out here, with Ella, and we want to come in.

About a half hour later we'd successfully summoned the manager of the co-op and were back at the house with a security guard and a passkey.

We rang again several more times and called out, again and again, before using the key, Phyllis and Ella back at the foot of the stairs, waiting, the three elderly women keeping watch with them. Rose, I called, stepping inside, it's me, David, with the security guard, and we're coming inside. But there was no reply, and no one seated either in the living room or in the den, where I turned off the television. Mom? I called again, Mom? as I stepped inside the bedroom, where she sat at a small roll-top desk, a thick album of photos open in front of her, a pool of loose photos at her feet. She did not look up when I approached her, but her eyes were open, and she held in one hand a pair of scissors, in the other hand half a photo, the irregular edge unmistakable there in the light thrown by the floor lamp just to her right. When I reached forward to take the scissors from her hand she pulled away and said please don't touch my hand, I'm asking you. I saw that the photos at her feet were half photos, that she'd obviously been sitting there for some time, coolly emptying the photo album, neatly slicing each picture and letting it fall. Her hair was freshly combed, and she wore, I could see, lipstick and eyeliner that had been freshly applied. Do you want me to? I began, but no, she interrupted, I want you to nothing. Can I tell Phyllis to come up the stairs with Ella? I need nothing from Phyllis and nothing from you, and definitely nothing from Ella. Not even for a little while? Not now. I'm telling you. If I want something I'll ask. You'll hear from me.

I dismissed the security guard then, told Phyllis to remain outside with the baby, and then checked the apartment. There was plenty of food in the refrigerator, and when I looked at the dates on the milk and eggs and juice I could see that my mother had been shopping within the past week. There were no unusual supplies of pills in either of the medicine cabinets, and in the hall closet I saw the month's supply of bottled water that had been delivered earlier in the month. If my mother was mad, she was selectively so. She shopped, she received deliveries, she turned on the television, and she made herself up as if she expected to see someone. Though she probably needed help, I did not know precisely what form that help would take, and I knew that anything I arranged would be unwelcome. Phyllis said I would blame myself if something terrible happened to her, but I said she deserved to make up her own mind about her life. When we drove away at last I thought it might be a very long time till I saw my mother again, and I was not at all unhappy about that prospect. She was pitiful, yes, but she had made up her mind, such as it was, to live as she was living, and I was going to live my own life with no less determination.

The last time I saw my mother was at our house. She had shown up unannounced on a late May Saturday afternoon, bearing a small box of Whitman's chocolates, her hair wrapped in a black head-scarf in spite of the unusually warm afternoon sun. Of course Phyllis invited her in, though she waved off Phyllis's attempt to embrace her, and refused the invitation to take off her scarf, or her red nylon bomber jacket. Come back to the kitchen, mom, Phyllis said. Ella's in the high chair. I'll stay out here, my mother said. You go take care of the baby. Take a seat at least, Phyllis said, and I'll call David. Da-vid, she shouted. You'll never guess who's here. And with that she walked briskly to the kitchen, glancing back at Rose, standing stiffly against the armoire in the entranceway, turning once more to say Rose, for god's sake, please sit down in the living room.

When I came down the stairs Rose remained standing, and turned her head away when I tried to kiss her. It's about time you came over, mom, I said, but why the hell didn't you call us?

Call you? she asked. Call YOU? Why would I call you? To disturb your holy family maybe? To hear your father's voice cooing at the baby, or maybe someone else's, who I half expected to see sitting on the porch with the baby on her lap? That's who I should call?

You're talking crazy, mom, I said. I mean it's how many years since dad left, and then the year with Sam in the apartment, and still you're carrying on about some big dramatic violation? And feeling hurt again, as if it happened yesterday, and you were the avenging angel, who can't look at her own granddaughter for who knows what insane reason?

Get me a glass of water, she said. Go on and get it, and bring it out here,

by the door, I won't go any further into your house. Her voice steady, her
eyes clear, no sign of weakness or impending apology, nothing soft or forgiving or appealing, nothing motherly. And so I turned without a word
and went to fetch the glass of water, Phyllis in the kitchen still with Ella,
somehow afraid to come back out to the entranceway, to confront again
that unforgiving countenance. But when I returned with the water I saw
that the door to the front porch was ajar, the box of chocolates on the floor,
and I rushed out in time to see Rose marching up the sidewalk, her leather
tote bag slung over her shoulder, the scarf tight on her head. I called to
her once only, from the porch, could not bring myself to run after her,
wanted not to see her turn back and look at me again with her clear cold
eyes.

About a half hour later the door bell rang. A young man in shorts and
a tee shirt asked if an elderly woman in a red silk jacket belonged—that's
the word he used—belonged to me, and when I said yes, she did belong
to me, he said well, then you ought to come out pretty quick, 'cause she's
lying down in the gutter down near the corner, and the cars are all backed
up, and no one can get her out of the way. And of course I went with him,
and sure enough, there was Rose, lying in the gutter with her arms rigid
at her sides, her legs straight out, as if she were performing a stretching exercise, her eyes wide open. As I approached her, glancing only for a moment at the six or eight onlookers assembled at the curbside, and said
Rose, please, just get up, get up now, she yelled, screamed, a loud, sustained scream, completely incomprehensible, a howl really, of pain, to be
sure, though I heard in it a note of anger, a declaration somehow, though
without words, that I was not to come any closer, so that when I did come
closer, and kneeled down as if to lift her, gently, she kicked at me, got me
in the shin first, then again struck my arm and my chest, the screaming
more furious still, and I looked around me, and did not know what to do,
what might be expected of me, and I began to back away. It occurred to
me, even then, with my leg hurting, and others clearly wondering at my
willingness to be backed away, that it was my duty to fling myself at her,

to hug her to me tenderly, even if kicking and screaming, and to beg her forgiveness, and to drag her if need be back to the house.

But I did not beg her forgiveness, did not again kneel down or implore her. I heard her scream again, and again, and I was afraid, and so I left her there, where she lay, stumbled back to the house and locked the door against her.

Samantha

She was angry. No one had told her to be, not in so many words, but she felt the rush of indignation, heard her voice tremble when she told the man to keep his explanations to himself. She had asked him a simple question, made a simple request, and he had refused her. That is all she needed to know and all she wanted to hear from him. His song and dance about inadequate staff and poor equipment, his complaints about having to put up with endless hassles — none of this seemed to her to have anything to do with her. She had asked him — a flunkey in the college's audiovisual department — to arrange for her a private screening of a film she was supposed to have seen with her class on Monday night, when she was just too tired to go out.

Now the charmless little man had turned her down, said it was impossible, and she was required to listen to him justify himself to her. He had stringy, probably unwashed red hair and an ugly little pointed beard. He wore, beneath a v-neck sweater, a button-down white shirt and an impeccably knotted silk necktie which she thought pretentious and ridiculous. He called her "Miss" and she thought the best thing she could do for him was to tell him to keep his reasons to himself. But she let him go on and finally said only that she didn't like the tone of his voice and did he know that he was rude? For a moment she liked the nervous shifting of his beady eyes after that, the way he sort of retreated, asked her to let him apologize for his rudeness — though he had not intended to be rude — but then almost at once she felt again the surge of raw anger and asked him to write for her his name and his extension number. Nor did she explain to him why she needed his name, or agree to let him apologize. When she grabbed the ragged scrap of paper from his twitchy hands she told him only that he should be more careful, jack, and that he'd be hearing from her. He didn't seem happy.

She had been feeling angry all week. Her roommate Sulema had told her she had a scowl on her face, and once or twice in class the other day she had heard herself raise her voice when she disagreed with something her history teacher had said. She had always been aggressive—that was an expression she liked, an expression that had been more than once applied to her—but she had usually thought herself nonetheless perfectly polite. She knew that others her age would have laughed at her way of admiring politeness, at her already long-standing hatred of rudeness and bad manners. But now she found herself raising her voice, inviting others to look at her as if she were one of those people always ready to explode, on edge, alert to any slight, impatient with anything contrary or dim. Her history teacher had not seemed to notice anything sharp in the tone of her voice. He followed up her harsh comments the other day as if they were conducting the most pleasant conversation in the world, disagreeing in the moment only to discover what well-bred professorial types like him would call common ground. Now those words on somebody's professorial lips made her want to puke. She didn't at all like this guy's way of suggesting that when all was said and done she'd see things his way. Someone should tell that boy to come off it. She noted with irritation how, the moment she loudly cleared her throat, he jotted something in his notebook, and she instantly wrote in her own notebook a reminder to ask the sucker what he'd written in that slick scented-paper pad of his.

The encounter with the guy at audiovisual left her feeling agitated. She walked out of the building and moved quickly across the green, failing to acknowledge the wave of a suite mate, not quite knowing what she was going to do. Someone has got to talk to that boy, she repeated to herself as she entered the college center and went down the stairs to the office of minority affairs. The walls in the corridor were as always plastered with notices announcing multicultural dinners, dances and discussions. Grievance meetings were scheduled on Wednesdays at 7. A specialist in English as a second language would be on campus every Monday. A fund-raiser for a new multicultural resource center was planned for late November.

She hated all this multicultural bullshit. They were building their own little world, she thought, and she was supposed to be grateful. More than once in the past she had wanted to tear down every one of these notices, to sit in one of the uncomfortable plastic chairs at the far end of the corridor and look at the expressions on the faces of the brothers and sisters when they arrived for work in the morning and saw the clean white walls, stripped of all that irrelevance. You'd have to be more than a little brainwashed, she thought, to buy into this stuff, into this pathetic little world with its Afro-American pride and its Latino heritage and its Asian-American feel-good fantasies. She had come down here not, she assured herself, because she had anything but contempt for all of this, but because she had a simple question to ask. If a sister could give her an answer, she'd just say thank you very much and depart. She wouldn't need to do more than that.

The sister at the desk, in fact, offered her a cup of coffee and insisted that Samantha sit down, though she said she was in kind of a hurry. She was in no mood to trade niceties with this flunkey, and she bristled when the sister noted that she'd never seen her "down here" before. And just why would she be expected to put in an appearance down here? she asked. Was this a requirement? Did every other black girl come in for a "periodic" chat? She had thought that might be the case, and that was why she'd stayed away for the two years she'd been at the school. Did the sister understand that? Whatever the problems students had, it was not a good thing for every black girl to take her ass on down to the same place to be handed the same kind of social worker jive. None of that, no way, not at the Concord Academy—you know it?—where she'd spent four years of high school without once being forced into some poor little black girl office. She had thought, having stayed away from this basement office for two whole years, and handled her own problems in her own way, that she might just come down to ask a simple question. But now she was sorry she had bothered, and she would bring her question to someone else, who didn't expect her to come in, and who wouldn't get all moist and excited about adding another name to their inventory of needy cases. Know what I mean? This ain't no affirmative action baby you got here.

The woman watched her with what looked like amazement. She was a big woman, with fleshy forearms and a wide nose. She leaned forward and gripped the ends of her desk with thick, angry hands. Samantha could see that she had hit a nerve, and for a moment she thought the woman might just ask her to get the hell out. But of course, Samantha thought, these social worker types never got that excited. She knew their kind. They were into control, soothing and control. Samantha was not surprised when the woman asked her to just state the problem, then, and to spare her all the anger. She did have a problem, didn't she?, or did she just come down to insult a sister? Samantha repeated that she should never have come, but took a chair and said, quietly, that a guy in audiovisual had been rude to her. Did he call her a name? the sister asked. No, he didn't call her a damn name. Did he make some reference to her race? No, of course he didn't. The sucker didn't have the balls to say anything like that straight out. And was there something in his tone she could identify? It was there, Samantha assured her, but she didn't think she could identify it, not exactly. And did she, perhaps, not speak first to the man with a certain obvious hostility of her own?

Samantha didn't like this question, and asked the sister what she meant. But the sister just stared silently at her for several seconds and then said she didn't think Samantha had much of a story. She asked for the name of the man in AV, wrote it down and reported that no one had ever complained to her about him before. Did Samantha want to file a formal complaint and have the man brought in? Or did she want to tell her more about it? Samantha said she'd think about it and let the sister know. Would a week be alright? The sister nodded. And would the sister drop the FM radio voice and stop treating the student sisters like helpless children? "You get the fuck out of here" was all Samantha heard before the woman heaved her large body out of the ample desk chair and left Samantha sitting by herself in the office.

Samantha heard the woman slam the door to the adjacent room and looked up at the idiotically out of place poster-size photograph of Nelson Mandela garbed in a colorful dashiki. Like the sister knew anything at all about the man, she thought. About anything. Like she was some goddamn revolutionary and not some overfed grievance collector. As she rose to leave she caught a glimpse of her own twisted scowl and neatly ironed white button down shirt in the fake eight by ten Victorian mirror propped on the sister's desk. She turned the glass face down and scrawled on the sister's appointment calendar "Samantha Bailey, extension 2465."

A few minutes later she left the campus and crossed the wide thoroughfare towards the familiar shop fronts. She headed for the Barnes and Noble superstore, a pained, weary expression on her face as she elbowed past the browsers massed at the remainder tables in the entranceway. Inside, she paused and put on a look of ferocious incredulity as she studied the titles arrayed on the wide shelves below the information counter. Stray fragments caught her eye, assailed her. They Can Kill You . . . How to Survive the Loss of Love . . . Race Matters . . . Cruel and Unusual . . . Good Boys . . . To The Friend Who Did Not Save . . . Again and again she looked over the "Staff Selections" titles. It seemed to her pathetic that anyone would take seriously these selections. Did anyone actually care what some bookstore flunkey recommended?

She looked around and saw a couple sit down heavily on the carpeted floor a few feet away and spread out in front of them what looked like a computer printout. The guy adjusted the glasses on the bridge of his nose while the girlfriend ran a finger down the long sheet. She wanted to ask them if they'd considered what the other customers were supposed to do with them blocking up the aisle. Was she supposed to fly over them? Or did the cozy pair think that no one would possibly be interested in the biographies shelved just past them, in a place no one could reach now that two fools were blocking the way? She didn't ask, of course. The two little darlings wouldn't know what hit them if she so much as breathed in their direction. Probably they'd smile nervously at her and quickly gather up their stupid mess. Then she'd want to hit them.

Not ten minutes later she stood in line at the counter waiting to buy a book of interviews with film directors. Her teacher had read excerpts from the book in class, and she found herself talking about the directors and their films more than anything else these days. Sulema couldn't understand what spoke to her so powerfully in those films, with their subtitles and their depressing melancholy. What was worse, far worse, Sulema complained, all but two of the directors they studied in their film class were white and male. At the register a clerk asked her if she had read the book of interviews with Scorsese, and Samantha asked him, "You ever read *The Magic Lantern?*" She didn't like the way the sissy-ass boy looked at her, but when she took her change she couldn't help telling him they should do a better job with the film books. For a big store they let their stock run down too damn fast. The boy muttered something about telling a manager, and she was out the door before he could say anything stupid.

She had moved up the sidewalk only eight or ten steps when she found herself face to face with slick Professor Rothstein. He smiled at her and held out his hand. This boy had all the moves. He asked her if she had found what she was looking for, and she said "apparently" as she held up the Barnes and Noble bag and waved it at him. Was she in a hurry? he wanted to know, and within a few seconds she had agreed to go back with him into the little café at the front end of the bookstore.

She looked around quickly to be sure no one she knew was watching. Inside they stood briefly together until they spotted an open table and moved to occupy the chairs. He bought her a cappuccino and a slice of zucchini bread and sat grinning across from her at the bright red table. She thanked him for the "treat" and stared at the long silver hair in his fine moustache. He wore his standard herringbone tweed jacket over a plaid flannel shirt open at the collar. He seemed comfortable, she noted, not over-friendly but wanting to connect. She had no idea what he thought he was doing, taking a student to a café, but she wasn't shy, and she just had to find out what this boy had on his mind. He was old enough to be her father, and in class often mentioned his wife and his daughter. Once he even said he'd seen the Bergman films when they first opened in New York twenty, thirty years earlier. With his shoulder-length hair and unruly beard he didn't much look like somebody's idea of a father, but he was more than starting to go gray, and his eyes seemed to her older than the rest of him. She noticed that he didn't in the least seem nervous with her, that he invited small talk, and that he drank his own cappuccino with undisguised pleasure. She was only momentarily surprised when he asked her "by the way" what he'd been meaning to ask her, whether she went to "a special place" to have her hair done "like that." It occurred to her that this might have been offensive, and that she might have ended their little chat before it even got started, but she told him calmly that she liked doing her dreadlocks for herself, and that it had taken her a long time to learn how to do them right. He said he could only faintly imagine how hard it was, and how much trouble it had to be to undo it all and give it a good wash. Was that part hardest of all? he asked.

"You're asking," she said, "do I wash my hair and undo all my hard work?"

"I mean," he said, betraying no sign of discomfort, "that people tell me you can't just routinely wash your hair if you want your hair like that."

"What kind of people tell you?" she demanded.

"I don't know," he replied. "More than one person."

"You talk a lot about girls with dreadlocks?" she asked.

"Not a lot," he said. "But it does seem to come up."

"They excite you?" she asked. "Maybe the fact you figure they're kind of dirty, unwashed and all, maybe that gives you a kind of thrill or something."

"I'm not talking about thrills," he said. "I think I'm able to like something without becoming excited, not that way. There is something to be said for disinterested liking."

"More or less disinterested," she corrected him. "We're not sitting together here in a café talking about the hair on the head of a Roman princess in some wall painting. We're talking about the hair on the head of an actual black girl in your own class."

"You have me there," he said, smoothing his beard. "Fair enough. Not altogether disinterested. But almost."

They went back and forth this way for almost a half hour, the professor only a bit more cautious, Samantha clearly delighted with her ability to tease him. "Seriously now," she said to him at one point, "how many times you talk about my locks?"

"If you want to know," he said, "I've mentioned them more than once to my daughter, Jennie, who's twelve. She thinks that's the way to do her own hair, which is kind of unruly, like a bird's nest that's seen a lot of action."

"You tell your daughter my name? You tell her I have a gold tooth in my mouth, up near the front?"

"I believe I've stuck to the dreadlocks."

"That's better," she said, "safer. Best not even to think about the tooth. Am I right?"

Here he looked briefly reluctant, stretched his legs out, moving slightly away from the table, from her, and she figured she'd hit a nerve, or something, threw him off, who could tell. And this boy thought he knew everything, thought there was nothing could surprise him, or not really.

But then he said, "Actually I have thought about the tooth. More than your hair, I mean. It's so, you know, surprising, in you. When you open your mouth and those tremendously sophisticated sentences roll out I find myself just staring at the tooth, not so you'd notice, but I do stare, so that it puzzles me afterwards. I mean, it doesn't exactly fit with the button-down white shirts and the, you know, expensive-looking shoes."

"Didn't figure I'd bring up the tooth, did you?" she asked.

"I wouldn't have wanted you to," he said. "Too hard a subject for either of us."

"Not hard for me," she said, "and so not really hard for you. Not if you're brave and all."

"I'm not brave actually," he said, "but now that you've opened it up, I can't very well run away, can I? And so I'll ask you right out, what the hell is going on with that tooth of yours?"

"You don't like it," she said. "I can hear it in your voice. It makes you a little sick just to think of it, doesn't it?"

"I never said I hated it," the professor replied. "On the contrary. It just seems to me so strange for a girl like you. I mean, I would have thought the family that sent you to, you know, Concord Academy and such places, and then to a place like this, that the family would just have said no, that tooth is out of the question."

"Well they did try to talk me out of it," Samantha said. "But I was defiant, and I'm nobody's sweetheart when I decide to say no, no way I'm gonna give something up."

"And so," he interrupted, "you insisted on the thing mainly because you knew it would drive your parents nuts."

"Not so," she said, smiling brightly and wagging her finger at him. "In a way my parents were, you know, negligible in the decision I made. It was freshman year, two years ago, and I had a tooth pulled. Painful, but simple. And then I thought, why not a gold tooth? I saw them on some kids in my neighborhood, and I thought, that's weird. Now, when I imagined a gold tooth shining there in my own mouth, it came to me: nobody, but nobody's gonna know what to do with that, and so why not? Didn't take me more than five minutes to decide. You know what I'm talking about? It's something, you know, unassimilable, and don't you like that word? Unassimilable? Nobody's gonna be able to do a thing with a tooth like that, except like it, or hate it. You can't use it, can't explain it. You can take it or leave it, but you can't give any reason for it. It's a thing, you know, beyond reason, if you know what I mean. You can't look at it and say, why that girl, she's got a nigger tooth in her head, 'cause you don't see a lot of black girls walking around with a tooth like that, not right up front. And if you're a black brother, you know, the kind who's not gonna sit here with you sipping a nice hot cup of cappuccino, you sure won't say, that Samantha, she studies hard and does what she's supposed to, and all because she wants to be white. You take one look at that tooth and you're sure this is one girl who sure doesn't wish she was white. No way. And that suits me, 'cause I sure don't want to be an ordinary defensive black girl, and I sure don't want to be white, 'cause there's no way I can pass, and there's no way I'm gonna look up to most of the white people I meet. Present company excluded, if you know what I mean. And you can stop looking so amazed, with your mouth open just enough to show me there's no gold tooth out there in the middle of your pretty white mouth."

They had by then been at it for more than an hour, the professor obviously content to bring her out, Samantha not in the least reluctant to take the lead and to stun him wherever possible, now a little flirtatious, now merely teasing. I got this boy right where I want him, she thought to herself now and again, not knowing really what she wanted or whether there was some further prospect in this exchange she would soon discern. But she felt an acute sense of disappointment when at last he looked at his watch and said it was getting very late. She had an impulse then to reach out and cover his wrist with her hand, and she was—she hoped not visibly—relieved when he asked if they shouldn't order "just one more drink." But then something, she didn't know what, came over her, and she said, simply, "No more drinks" and "I think we've had enough for now, don't you?" and "Don't want to make too much of a good thing, now do we?" And with that, he said, "You're right," and "Thank you, Samantha," and they got up together to go out.

Through the large windows she could see that darkness had fallen, and she noted that several students had stood browsing nearby among the foreign newspapers and quarterly magazines. She no longer cared, quite the contrary, that they might be noticed leaving together, but she was mildly irritated by one student who kept looking her over and maybe even straining to catch what she and Rothstein were saying to one another. Samantha wouldn't give her the satisfaction of lowering her voice, no way, and she saw that Rothstein took no notice of anyone else as he helped her on with her jacket. She liked the half smile she caught on his face, thought he licked his lips when he felt her arm slide into the jacket sleeve.

On the sidewalk outside he reached forward to shake her hand, but she laughed, a short, abrupt, nervous laugh, and held onto his fingers much longer than was usual, held onto them and said, finally, "Now that's not so bad, is it?" And then she released him, and brazenly blew him a kiss as he backed away and turned to retrieve his car.

When she played it back to herself that night, over and over again, she thought: not wise, not prudent at all, but she couldn't decide whether the words applied to Rothstein or to herself. Was there, she wondered, some drama of sexual subjugation unfolding in there, Rothstein somehow pretending to be cool and, like he said, dispassionate, or disinterested, but in fact communicating all the while his desire and counting on her to pick up the cues? Was the whole thing a seduction, Samantha herself the improbably manipulable object, swollen with pride at her own command of the situation but deceived, oh yes deceived, by the man who never doubted, not once, that he had her where he wanted her? It wasn't easy to sort this out, she thought, not with all those weird convolutions, those thickets of improbability. She had been, no doubt about it, caught up in something there, all afternoon removed from her usual sense of self, not bitter at all, not sniffing around to spy the moves she thought she'd learned to spot from a mile away. But this boy, he had the moves, had them down so well even she couldn't make them out, not till they had worked their way with her, as she now felt, reduced her to a kind of confusion she didn't at all recognize or like. She liked the man, of course, and that was a big part of the problem. She liked the way he listened to her and said she was sophisticated and all, the way not a lot of others would dare say to her face. And for that matter, who else ever would tell he couldn't stop thinking about her tooth? Who else? Though just that was a sort of sign, wasn't it, that he wanted to tell her something more, you, know, dangerous, without having to put it out there in so many words?

And yet she had very abruptly put an end to their flirtatious afternoon, as if she had not at all enjoyed what was happening and wanted just to get the hell out of there. Was she, suddenly, afraid that he might go on to say something really imprudent, something she would have to count as offensive? Was she trying, without quite knowing it, to prevent him from spoiling the little thing they had managed between them, something small and, when you came right down to it, incorrigibly innocent? She liked that sort of expression when she read it in a book or when, unbidden, it crossed her mind, liked the knotted, tangled up contradictoriness of the thing, its heading two or more ways at the same time. And that was what she was feeling at this strange juncture, that she had just participated in something heading off in several apparently irreconcilable directions, teasing and sort of affectionate, innocent and strangely seductive, ordinary and, in a way she didn't grasp at all, elemental.

Had she hoped, she wondered, or half hoped, that he would make some further move? When she put her hand out on the table right under his nose, stretched her arm out there so that he might almost have thought she was reaching for his hand, idly passing back and forth over the rim of the cup, did she hope or expect that he would in fact take hold of her hand? Now that would have been something, she thought. And would he have known that, had he done that simple thing, it would have seemed to her objectionable, even if she wanted him to do no less? Oh she could see herself—even with her revulsion at the thought that he was somehow taking advantage—could see herself going off somewhere with Rothstein if he invited her, said to hell with the fact that he was expected at home and simply proposed that they, you know, spend the evening somewhere together. It wasn't so ridiculous, not really, to imagine herself with this man. She could imagine worse things than letting him do her while they lay together somewhere watching a video of *Wings of Desire*. Sure she might have wanted, all the while, to haul his sweet improper ass into some hearing room to file a complaint against him for what would surely seem to anyone a grown man's abuse of his professorial authority. But that part, about hauling his ass into more trouble than that boy had ever seen, that part she didn't know about. Not really sure what she would have done. There was something she didn't like, never liked, about the coercive, inescapable indignation young women like herself had been made to hold at the ready, suspicious always of anyone, any man, who liked them, and suspicious too of themselves and of what had been done to them when they felt their throats tighten in expectation of some implacable sexual excitement. She was, she felt, excitable, sensual, but she didn't at all like to think of herself as a girl who could be seduced. Not certainly by an older man practiced in seduction. This boy Rothstein had that air about him, though he sure as hell didn't give too much of it away.

Later that night, impatient for her dorm mate Sulema to come in, and unable to read or write, she showered, but left the bathroom door open, expecting—it was stupid, sure—that he would maybe phone her. Had she left her number? Of course she hadn't. But he was a bright boy. He would know how to look up her number. And what would he say if he did call? That he had a question to ask her about *Chloe in the Afternoon?* That he was taking a shower and couldn't get her dreadlocks or her gold tooth out of his mind? That she should come right on over and have a friendly chat with his wife, or help his daughter with her hair?

By the time she emerged from the shower and stood squeezing a tiny, ugly grey pimple on her left cheek, she knew he couldn't call. Not if he wanted to. Not if he could read her mind. Especially not if he could read her mind. He wasn't careful, that was sure, but he wasn't stupid either. She'd read often enough that men as old as Rothstein became easily infatuated with younger women. Often they were—she liked this expression—sexually inebriated in the presence of girls young enough to be their daughters. They obsessed a lot. That Russian guy Nabokov knew about this better than anyone. Rothstein might be such a guy. Maybe he told himself he was interested in her mind. Maybe he liked what she had to say about the movies. But he'd noticed her hair, couldn't stop thinking about her tooth. He hadn't taken his hand away, had he, when she grazed his knuckles? She seemed to recall that there had been such a moment. And there was no stiffening or look of aversion on his face when she threw him that kiss—a daughterly kiss, maybe, but no, he could tell it was more intimate than that. It couldn't have been lost on a bright boy.

She wanted Sulema to come home. Possibly she would tell her nothing, or at least not more than a part of what had happened. But she wanted to make up her mind about a few things, and she couldn't decide how much to tell until Sulema stood there. She dried her hair and several times said into the mirror shit, Sulema, where the fuck are you? She applied alcohol to her pimple with a cotton ball and put on a CD of *Bachillanas Brassilleras* she'd owned since that music teacher played it for the class that time in high school. The soprano voice always seemed to her unearthly and exalted. She tried to sit and listen but found herself restless and strangely exhilarated. She moved around the little apartment, from one corner to another, and only realized when she stood in front of the tall window in the kitchen that she hadn't dressed. She ran back to her room and took a plush white terry-cloth robe from the hook behind her door.

By 11:15, really angry now with Sulema for staying out so late, and with herself for giving a damn, she phoned Professor Rothstein and heard a woman pick up and ask in a faint husky voice who it was. Samantha said nothing, but breathed loudly enough to be sure the woman would know someone was there. The woman asked her husband to try, and when Samantha heard him say hello, who is it, is anybody there? she hung up and turned off the kitchen lights.

The next day, early, she noted with disgust that Sulema had stayed out all night, probably shacked up with some twenty-year-old half-wit. She dressed quickly and went out for breakfast at the dining hall on campus. For some reason she couldn't remember the name of the woman down at the minority affairs office, the phony sister of mercy who'd finally exploded at her, as she was bound to do. But that was no matter. She could easily find her way to the office and look up the name in a directory. No doubt the sister would remember the name of one Samantha Bailey. But there was every reason to doubt she'd know what to do with the information Samantha intended to set before her now. Would she conclude, pretty much the way she did the other time, that the behavior described was, you know, how that writer put it in his book, not sufficiently reprehensible? Samantha helped herself to a bowl of muesli and vanilla yoghurt and tried to picture the professionally concerned look on the face of that perfect hand-holding political correctness machine seated complacently down there surrounded by all those comforting icons of struggle. She searched her mind for the conscientious jargon words the sister would spread around to soothe her troubled spirit. Even if she could not find sufficient cause in anything Samantha told her to bring formal charges against the Professor, she would surely find ways to say the right things and to nurture at least the capacity for sustained indignation.

Samantha drank a second cup of less-than-acceptable coffee and was tickled by the observation that, as usual, she had the table all to herself, though any number of students known to her had passed nearby and failed to greet or join her. Out on the campus green she closed her parka tight against the wind and put out her tongue to taste a blowing snowflake or two. She walked on the covered walkway around the periphery of the green and made the circuit not once but three times. She was seized by a powerful desire to speak to Rothstein, to tell him something he would not be able to ignore. But first she would ask him what he meant to say the other day when he confided to her that he often thought of her gold tooth. Was that some sort of sign or message he intended her to pick up? She could excuse that, she would say, so long as he was in fact—how best to say this?—interested in her, not really or solely in the fact of her tooth, or the hair, or her curiously unstable classroom demeanor, but in her, her, in which case she would have no trouble at all saying that she understood and would try as hard as she could to reciprocate that interest. To tell the truth, she had once or twice acknowledged to herself that she was interested in him, and well before the time they had spent together in the café.

As she made her way slowly around the campus walkway it seemed to her that she was getting nowhere with her fantasies, getting nowhere with Rothstein. Why should such a man be drawn to a black girl like herself? What indication had he given, that she should construct such fantasies of reciprocal intensity? There was, she felt, though she was not at all sure how to put it to herself, something more than Rothstein himself at the bottom of the powerful attraction she was allowing herself to feel. It was not, she was certain, a father-thing she was feeling, a displaced affect of the kind she'd read about in a psych class. No, it was something more power-ful, more openly sexual. And it had, she was sure, something also to do with the sister waiting ever so patiently, massively, down in that unspeak-ably virtuous basement office. To go to Rothstein, she felt, would be to do something good and necessary, whether he was glad to see her or not, afraid of her or willing to have a dangerous fire lit under him. Not to seek out Rothstein, to go instead to see the sister, would be to betray something in herself. That she knew, though there was, just as surely—she could taste it—the usually surging, corrosive indignation she knew so well and, until very recently, fully trusted. She was, it seemed, in the grip of some-thing new, some urge to say no, no to the big sister, no to some idea of pro-priety and to the settled suspicion of malfeasance. This suspicion she knew to be somehow alien to her, though she had not the words to say ex-actly how, not alien or corrosive merely but stupid and shallow.

Was she a confused young black girl with ideas too big for her to han-dle? She said to herself again and again that yes, she was young and con-fused and in over her head. And then, having repeated this to herself, and completed a final circuit of the campus green, she went to Rothstein's office and, seeing that he wasn't expected in at all on this day, she sat in the department secretary's office and wrote him a short note. It said: "Samantha Bailey is very grateful for the interest you have shown her and patiently awaits your call (evenings, extension 2465). At your leisure, at your discretion."

She slid the note under Rothstein's office door, then, standing outside the door in the dark corridor, wrote another note, this one addressed to "Director, Office of Minority Affairs." It read: "Samantha Bailey of the Ju-nior class wishes to inform you that she is presently involved with a white Professor, and if you don't believe that is at all appropriate, you can either kiss my perfect black ass or offer me an explanation that doesn't conde-scend or repeat the standard stupefying bullshit. I may be reached most evenings at extension 2465. You can leave me a message if you must, but it had better be damn good if you expect me to answer it. And no, I am definitely not yours very truly, SB."

A Perfect Stranger

Who did you think you were? From the first moment I wanted to ask you. The guy next to me said you were an idiot, and for an instant I thought he was right. You did seem more than a little deranged just then, in spite of your expensive seat, your white panama hat and your gaudy silk cravat. Had anyone before you, I wondered, ever removed two rows of people, forced them from their seats, so rapidly and violently? Anywhere? Let alone at Tanglewood, with hundreds of nearby spectators gaping, astonished, incredulous? When you think of it, it's a wonder no one got up to stop you, strange that you never paused to reconsider, never signalled to the kids you pulled from their seats to come back, that it was all a joke, a momentary fit of pique, an aberration.

I didn't know then—I think I know it now—that you were not much on apologies or regrets, didn't know, not at first, what I thought of you. But from the moment I followed you out to the parking lot, past the tall birches and the festive green awnings, I knew I wanted something from you I couldn't name, and I imagined you were a man made for dangerous feats.

Like everyone else in section three at Tanglewood that Sunday afternoon, I'd heard the commotion well before you swung into action. I'd heard the shushings and murmurings of disapproval throughout the opening Dvořák Sonatina, and leaned forward two or three times to glare at the kids talking and laughing and whistling as if Perlman and Ax were not struggling to be heard in a shed designed not for intimate chamber pieces but for orchestral performance. I saw you leave your seat after the first movement and whisper something to an usher before returning. I remember that you stood up again after the second movement, and that you spoke sharply to the kids, raising your voice to warn a few of the noisier creatures. It occurred to me that these were residents of a summer camp, most of them fourteen or fifteen years old. Obviously they had no interest in chamber music and would have preferred an afternoon at the lake.

It seemed to me odd that so many of them—sixty or seventy—should have been deposited in two long rows of seats with no adult supervision. But no counsellor or attendant rose at any point to reprimand them, and anyone could have predicted that the kids would grow even more unruly. It was predictable that program covers would be made into airplanes and launched, that at least a few kids, one of them directly in front of you, as I recall, would stand on their chairs and whistle or pretend to conduct the performers. I almost laughed when that straw hat was plucked from the head of our blue-haired senior citizen and passed around until it sailed— gracefully, don't you think?—up the center aisle.

Of course it occurred to me that any one of us might put an end to the commotion by grabbing one of the kids and shaking him for a second or two. But the suddenness of your thrust took all of us by surprise. I saw you step into the aisle and throw your sportscoat on the seat, and I stood up— I couldn't help myself—when I saw you grab the first kid and throw him into the aisle. The kids were immediately quiet, and we heard you yell "out" and "out" and "no, just shut up" and "I don't care" and "out," as one after another they were seized and thrown, first one row and then another, the kids mostly frightened and putting up less and less resistance, some fleeing over their friends away from you and up the aisle before you could reach them. Did you notice that none smiled, that some broke into tears—I heard them from my seat—boys as well as girls? Did it occur to you to wonder what they must have been thinking as they approached the top of the amphitheater and heard the applause, the scattered shouts of approval, as you returned to your seat and prepared to wait with the rest of us for Perlman and Ax to come back out for the Beethoven?

At the intermission I watched you closely, calmly observed the park guards and camp counsellors descend upon you. I liked the way your finger jabbed and pointed as you spoke, and your voice broke loudly over our heads as you refused to be cowed or admonished. No, you would not "step" in the direction of the manager's office. No, you would not apologize to anyone, certainly not to the children, and yes, if they returned to their seats and made a single sound, you would remove them again, along with their "idiot" counsellors.

"I'm afraid you'll have to talk about this with the manager," a park guard repeated, but you banished him with the threat that hundreds of your "neighbors"—you waved at us vaguely as you referred to us—would surely want to join you and to receive refunds for their tickets. "That's money I'm talking about here, do you see? That's trouble. And I don't go quietly."

Several people came over to shake your hand just before the musicians returned to the stage twenty minutes later. You seemed willing enough to accept their handshakes and to thank them for their approval. But you didn't want to strike up a conversation or respond to questions. When I asked if you had any kids of your own, you smiled noncommittally as if you were a public official accustomed to practicing discretions obscure to everyone else. You tended to look away when others tried to meet your eye, and I thought it odd that you betrayed no other signs of embarrassment. You didn't know it, but I couldn't take my eyes off you after that. I stared at your back throughout the Debussy sonata at the end of the concert, and when you rose to leave, I rose. I let you pass me in the aisle on your slow walk out of the amphitheater, and I waited for you outside the men's room, keeping my distance as if I'd been following a suspected criminal or someone who might be alarmed by my presence. I was aware of the bodies pressing now and then against me, of the programs littering the lawns and benches, of the overflowing trash receptacles and the hum of persistent conversation. I felt the late afternoon sun on my face and rolled up the sleeves of my damp linen shirt. Mostly I thought of what I would do when we reached the sprawling parking areas. Would you welcome a request for your name and phone number? You would think me dangerous, mad, as mad possibly as many of us had thought you at first. But I had no choice. To try to follow you was out of the question. Our cars would inevitably be parked at a great distance from one another. By the time I saw you get into yours it would be too late to find my own and catch up.

I approached you as you fumbled in your pocket for the keys to your car. You seemed at once to recognize me from the concert, and when you said, simply, yes, can I help you?, I couldn't but be grateful. Of course, I said, you can help simply by giving me your name, so I can tell people who it was that cleared all of those people out of their seats.

"They were kids," you said. "Maybe you're making too much of it."

But I persisted, and you gave in, writing for me your name and address in Northampton—the phone number was unlisted, you explained—and shaking my hand as you prepared to drive off. I liked the stately black Honda Prelude, and I noted the slender box of CDs you drew from the glove compartment and placed next to you. "I'll write to you," I promised as you smiled and pulled away, the parking lot rapidly emptying around us and me wondering whether I'd ever use the address you gave me.

As I drove home not fifteen minutes later I felt myself flushed and embarrassed, pictured myself, a stupid grin on my face, walking up to you, a perfect stranger, with a request for your name and address. The best thing I could do, I thought, was to tear up the paper you'd handed me and forget about looking you up. I imagined you at home in what I took to be a modest residence, on a tree-lined street a short walk from the center of town. I'd been in Northampton several times, once dated a girl from Smith College, and I remembered a good Thai restaurant I supposed you knew. Living in such a place you'd have been exposed to the varieties of genteel possibility there, and wouldn't at all have been surprised if I'd come onto you, even in so unlikely a setting as Tanglewood on a crowded summer afternoon. You couldn't know, of course, that coming on to you was the last thing I'd have wanted, that my wife was about as much as I could handle and that I looked to you for something else altogether. Really I had no way of knowing what you might offer, but the prospect of something important seemed irresistible. I saw myself for a moment with your colorful cravat tied firmly around my neck and deftly parrying insults as if nothing could be more natural. I liked the deep, gravelly timbre of your voice and thought for a moment that I might bring you an elegant walking stick when I came to call in Northampton.

The house was predictably quiet when I got back to Albany. My wife was away on a week-long camping trip with her sister, and I knew immediately what she'd say if I told her about our brief encounter. She'd be right, of course, to warn me that you were probably unstable, a person from whom almost anything might be expected. I looked at her picture on my desk in the study, and was pleased that I couldn't reach her just then on the phone. Undoubtedly I'd have blurted out everything, describing in detail your rampage through the teenage campers, but finding myself at a loss for words when I came to the part about my pursuit of you. Then she'd tell me to wait, just wait, and soothe me with words of love and the promise that she'd be home in just four more days. She'd even promise to come with me on the trip to Northampton, if I couldn't restrain myself and just had to go ahead with my plan.

At the Mac on my desk I opened a new file and began a document called "What Do I Want?," but I found my thoughts vague and erratic. I reached back to close the shades behind me, as if afraid that someone might be standing outside at the window, looking in at the inane fragments I put up on the screen. "Companionship," I wrote, and "risk," but I had no idea where to go with these. My wife had been my companion for nine years. I had colleagues, two brothers, friends I saw for dinner or movies on weekends. So far as I knew, I had no particular need of new companions. Neither had I previously shown an appetite for risk, or a notable lack of self-confidence. I was as decisive as the next man. I looked, now and then, at other women, and once or twice allowed myself to imagine, sharply, that my wife was attracted to a colleague, that she had reason to be tempted. Though I was hardly an adventurer, I had the nerve at least to see things as they were.

I woke early the next morning and decided not to go to work. I made myself some coffee, shaved, put on a fresh shirt and called the office. In the car within a few minutes I drove east towards the Mass Turnpike, entering Northampton on Route 9 ninety minutes later. I parked just outside of town across from the Smith College Admissions office. The tall trees had already begun to shed some leaves, but there was no sign of autumn color or of student activity on the sidewalks or campus greens. I'd no idea where Park Street was, or whether I'd have to get in my car again and drive there, but I strode calmly into the Admissions office and asked for directions. Park Street was about six blocks away, and I decided to walk.

The air was warm, but a light breeze was blowing, and for a few blocks I enjoyed myself. I surveyed the nineteenth-century houses with their manicured lawns and noted that many of the older, taller trees were scored with a broad, yellow X. I remembered earlier walks in the center of Northampton, where I shopped for second-hand books and drank espressos in small cafés. Someone had told me that the city had a large gay population, but it seemed to me no different from other college towns I knew. A mailbox with a name very much like yours reminded me that I was in pursuit of you and that I didn't know what I was doing. That thought should have frightened me a little, but having come this far, I was almost amused at my own stupidity, and detached enough to think I'd at least come away with a good story—though no one would believe me.

The house was pretty much as I had imagined it. There were handsome birches on the lawn, and the porch held several comfortable-looking wicker chairs. The windows were open, and the long lace curtains fluttered anxiously in their frames. I stood in the street, unwilling to step onto the sidewalk, and I listened for the sound of a radio or of voices within the house. After a minute or two, I strolled slowly around the side of the house, peering in at what looked like a breakfast room, but stopping at the fence to your back yard. There was an elegant chaise lounge, beside it a neatly painted white table holding a vase of cut flowers. There were

no signs of children, of tricycles or plastic pools or basketball hoops hung
over garage doors. All was orderly and trim, an adult world much like others I'd seen, but complete, somehow, in a way I'd not expected. I wanted
almost painfully to be inside, to run my fingers over the spines of your
books and to check out the range of your music library. I wanted to note
what you'd hung on the walls, and what kinds of chairs you'd chosen to
sit in. I was in search, so it seemed to me, of the reserves of quiet and
confidence you drew upon when you needed to.

Of course you were not at home. It was a Monday, and I figured you
were at work, in spite of the sultry summer days and the vacationing rev-
ellers carousing in Northampton every night. If you were married your
wife would probably have been at work too, though I saw no signs of a wife,
no distinctly feminine touches in the windows or in the decoration of the
house, which was a stolid Greek revival structure painted an impeccable
antique white. It occurred to me that I ought to look at the mailbox, but I
decided to wait until the mail was delivered a little later in the morning,
when I'd not risk an encounter with the mailman. I was inclined at one
point to enter the back yard and wait patiently for you. But that might take
all day, and so I walked around the block two or three times instead.

After lunch—briefly I drove into town for a burger and salad—I returned to the house, parking a block away and surveying the street to make
sure no one was watching me. The mailbox was crowded, I discovered,
drawing out a handful of envelopes and closing the box quietly behind
me. I had no intention, at first, of opening your mail, and would have been
appalled at the suggestion that I'd stolen anything or sought to invade your
privacy. But once I held the envelopes in my hands, an irresistible urge
came over me. I noted that everything was addressed to you, that there
was no reference to a "Mrs." or to anyone else, and I felt a sense of relief
that seemed to me alarming and absurd. Perhaps I thought things would
be easier, less complicated, if there were no one else to get in our way.

In any case, I held the mail tenderly in my hands for a few minutes before making my way to your back yard again. I sat at the white table with
the cut flowers and used one of my shoes as a paperweight to be sure the

envelopes did not blow away. I looked around casually and must have felt that, if I were caught in the act, I'd say that I was opening your mail for you and examining it to see if I might offer any help. The incredible arrogance and presumption of the response would be nicely balanced by the intimate and cozy way I'd insinuated myself into your territory. Where there was nothing furtive, perhaps, nothing would seem sinister or otherwise reprehensible.

In fact, I opened but a single piece, a sympathy card from "Clara" which contained only a printed message and a faint signature. The deep red envelope had not been properly sealed, and I got the card out without damaging or tearing anything. Of course I did not know to what loss Clara referred, but I suspected that you'd tell me at once, without my having to ask. I had no interest in Clara, who was content to be represented by a standard formula of condolence. You seemed too young to have a deceased wife, though I knew women of forty, or even younger, who had struggled with cancer and succumbed. It seemed to me unfair that I should have to wait much longer for you to tell me what I wanted to know. No doubt other pieces of mail I'd taken from your letterbox would clarify things a bit, but then it was possible they'd suggest further questions. The prospect irritated me, and I determined to put the envelopes back when I was ready to get up from your table. The cut flowers before me had no scent, but I was content just to stare at them and occasionally to study the return addresses on the personal letters lying there unread. I took off my other shoe, then my socks, and felt the cool grass between my toes. At one point an elderly neighbor greeted me breezily over the fence, and I waved to her without saying a word.

At four o'clock I expected you to return and to ask me what the hell I was doing in your yard with my shoes off. But you didn't come, and by five I found myself pacing, pulling up weeds along the fence and wondering how long it had been since you'd trimmed the hedges. I walked down a few steps and looked through a rear cellar door, but saw only a modest work table littered with wooden hammers and a length of copper wire. An old-fashioned saw hung on the wall. Nothing seemed to me to reveal any-

thing about you. Did you like to work with your hands? Had you bought
a house already outfitted with tools you would never use or know how to
handle? I supposed that you would be good at anything you set your mind
to, that you would be drawn, at least, to humble tasks, even if you did not
often perform them. But these speculations, like others preceding them,
were not particularly satisfying. I had passed a largely uneventful afternoon, and I was not much closer to you than I had been the evening before on the drive back from Tanglewood.

By six I decided you had made an evening appointment and would not
return until later. I was hungry, thirsty, and unaccountably angry. If I
waited for you into the night, you would think me a thief, or worse, and
our relationship might never recover from that initial impression, or from
the surge of fear my presence would probably inspire. I resolved to leave
before darkness fell, disgusted at the waste of a day, disappointed that you
had not somehow known that I was waiting and hurried home to greet me.
I stood on tiptoe looking in again at the side windows of the house, but
my eyes took in only dim shapes and the dull gleam of countertops. There
were two injured moths on the window ledge, and as I brushed them with
my elbow I grasped the screen handles on both sides and felt the screen
smoothly lift. I dragged a lawn chair across the grass to help me climb up
to the sill, and I stepped into the kitchen before I could ask myself, again,
what I was doing.

My eyes adjusted quickly to the dim interior, and I thought it best not
to turn on any lights. It did not occur to me that I was doing anything
wrong, or dangerous, though of course I would have been as alarmed as
you if I'd heard your key turn in the lock and we'd found ourselves unex-
pectedly face to face. I was conscious of endangering nothing, of explor-
ing calmly, almost meekly, as if I'd entered an obscure temple and intended simply to take an inventory of the artifacts and perhaps light a
candle on my way out. I was possessed by a determination to cover the
ground thoroughly, and I imagined you walking me through the recesses
of the place with equal determination.

It was not hard to suppose there would be signs of you everywhere, once I got past the nondescript kitchen with its predictable appliances and black and white tile floor. Though there were no pictures on the kitchen walls, no calendars or magnetic messages affixed to the refrigerator, I opened the cupboards for tell-tale signs and was surprised to find nothing but spices and a few boxes of linguine. It was as if you'd been away on vacation and had not yet replenished your supplies. It was conceivable, of course, that you routinely ate out, though people who occupied such houses in such places typically knew the pleasures of home cooking and ordinary domesticity. For some reason I would have been disappointed to find in you someone who kept no food and prepared no meals for himself. When I looked inside the refrigerator and found only a six-pack of Heineken and a half-drunk bottle of Perrier I hurried past the dining room and up the stairs to check the bedrooms.

The door to what looked like the master bedroom was half open, and I peered in to see the bed neatly made and the shades drawn. A black, somewhat battered steamer trunk stood at the foot of the bed. Though I could not bring myself just then to step into the room, I noted that there were no photographs on the walls and that the surfaces of the dresser and chests were empty. A black leather jacket lay folded across the seat of a ladder-back chair, but no other object caught the eye or excited the slightest interest. The room was without adornment, charm or color, the bedspread a pale rose, the wall fixture stark and functional.

The other upstairs rooms were comparably stark and unforgiving. The desk in the den held no papers, and the bookshelves contained a mostly random assortment of paperbacks, college texts and dictionaries. An old World Book Encyclopedia filled the bottom shelves of one bookcase in the corridor, and two worn copies of *Yankee* magazine rested on the tank of the toilet in the bathroom. A spare bed in a small room was covered only by a threadbare blanket. The closets smelled of camphor, and clothes were hung in carefully sealed plastic bags. I allowed myself, as I entered each room, to be struck by the absence of images or keepsakes, signs of affection or affiliation. I longed for something personal, an eccentric detail, an embroidered pillow or monogrammed towel, anything that might speak of an appetite, an assertion of preference or identity. Your desk contained bill stubs, an old credit card statement and a variety of pencils and paper clips, but there were no envelopes or signs of a correspondence, nothing received or waiting to be sent.

There was a sound system in the living room, but the few upholstered pieces were draped with sheets, and there was no sign of records, cassettes or a CD collection. Briefly I turned on a small table lamp to examine the contents of drawers in the television cabinet, but they held only a few wooden coasters and a set of pale yellow place mats. The television set was unplugged, like the receiver in the music system, and I looked in vain for anything resembling a hand-carved nutcracker, a bronze statue, a painted bird. When I turned off the light, vaguely aware that it might be noticed on the sidewalk outside, I sat heavily in a sheeted armchair and thought that this could not possibly be your house, that somehow a mistake had been made. I had climbed into the wrong house, investigated the wrong rooms. Oh yes, the name on the bill stubs was the name you had given me, but suppose you had sent me to someone else's house, given me someone else's name. Suppose you lived not in Northampton but in Amherst, or Pittsfield, or Williamstown, or someplace much bigger, Boston or Springfield. Suppose it had been your intention—conceived just then, in the parking lot, on the spur of the moment—to baffle a friend or acquaintance while eluding me altogether. Suppose you had seen, in my eyes, a hunger menacing in its lack of proportion or direction. You would surely have been wise, just then, to send me to someone else I might follow, to let me stew in my own avid juices.

For a while I revolved such thoughts bitterly, and I thought it might be best to settle things by parking my car in front of your house and waiting for you to come home. I would catch a glimpse of you as you turned into the driveway towards the garage. I would be sure. Seeing you, knowing you to be the occupant of this house, I would return to Albany prepared to write to you as planned, to arrange a meeting and pose questions. If someone else should appear in your place, I would leave and reconsider my options. I would deal with my anger, remember the several exasperations of this day, and try not to seek retribution. I would do my best to forebear and be gentle, to forgive, as you had not forgiven the children you drove from their seats, or the young people saddled with their care.

The sky had darkened a little by the time I went out the back door, crossed the garden, and walked up the sidewalk in front of your house. I kept going as I passed my car and stopped at a local deli for a sub and a soda. Outside a half hour later I felt myself pass rapidly from an almost giddy laughter to anger. Of course it seemed to me, even then, a preposterous course I had entered on. I had put myself in the way of disappointment. I had allowed myself to grow angry over imagined slights. I wanted to throw something, to smash one of your windows, at least overturn one of those shiny trash cans lined up under an awning alongside your garden. Seething, I stood as still as an idol, on a sidewalk not far from your house, and I resolved to get back to my car and drive away as quickly as I could. The darkening sky irritated me with its slowness. I wanted the blackness to come and swallow everything, to dry up every leaf on every tree.

In the car I knew myself capable of a malice I had not known before, and as I gripped the wheel I felt it bite into me, burn me like an acid. I breathed deeply and turned on the car radio to calm myself. Soon I returned to your street, circling, cruising slowly past the house, the car windows down, my eyes alert for any sign of you. Softly I played the radio, slowly I circled, until at ten I heard the familiar, soothing accents of Garrison Keillor reminding us that in Lake Wobegone all of the children are above average. At 11 I turned off the engine and sat across from your driveway listening to the night gathering around me. I heard, once or twice, a dog bark, but nothing moved on the street, and some time later I dropped the seat back and slept.

Do you know what it's like to wake up at 5:30 in the morning, your skin damp, the windshield cloudy before your eyes, your neck so stiff you can't turn it, but with your mind racing, convinced that, whatever you might decide to do, it will instantly strike you as the wrong thing, and worse than that, the thing you positively didn't want to do? Once or twice in the past

I'd demonstrated, or so I felt, a taste for melodrama, but here I really astonished myself, at once awake, besieged, beating myself up with idiotic, barely suppressed exclamations like "I'll wait here until you goddamn get back no matter how long it takes" and "if it turns out you sent me to someone else's place I'll make you pay" and "if you only knew what you're putting me through." I didn't wait long to dismiss these thoughts as the ravings of a person who had suffered a disappointment and passed a dark and uncomfortable night. Checking to be sure that no one had slipped into the driveway as I slept, I straightened up, drank a bit of Sprite from the can I'd nearly finished the night before, and drove off.

Clearly—I know you can understand this—I was in no mood to think of you then with love or gratitude or even with the sick longing I'd been feeling for more than twenty-four hours. I drove slowly, found myself sticking to the right lane of the turnpike, noting the cars passing me on the left, in no hurry to get anywhere, but eventually turning off at the Lee exit and idling alongside a brown athletic field parched from the long summer drought. It was early, no one on the field, and I saw in the distance what looked like two small boys stroking tennis balls in a leafier part of the facility. I left the car in a parking area behind home plate and walked aimlessly over second base, out into center field in the direction of the tennis courts. The balls hummed dully in the distance, and I thought unaccountably that I was a man who had not yet begun to live in the world. I was still quite far from the boys when I saw three other kids— they looked a lot bigger—descend on them from bicycles deposited on the grass not ten steps from the edge of the courts. They moved swiftly, without misgiving or fear, and loudly—I could hear their already resonant adolescent voices—demanded the tennis racquets. I continued to approach them, at once interested, and I saw the one with dark spiked hair roughly grab the smallest boy. You were, suddenly, in my mind—I'm sure of it—when I picked up my pace and hurried around to the courts on the far side of the high chain link fence that had separated me from the action. For a moment they took note of me, but by the time I got to them one of the boys had been knocked to his knees, the other stood unavailing at the net, and their three assailants were already back at the bicycles, tennis racquets in hand.

You will believe me when I say that it was not necessary just then to decide what to do, that I did not even for a moment reflect. I picked up from the soft ground a large rock and cradled it in my hand as I ordered the boys to put down the racquets — "Come on, put down the goddamn racquets," I commanded, steeling my voice as well as I could, "come on, put the racquets down and just get the hell away from here." But they looked at me without alarm, with what might have been contempt. One of them softly put down his bike again and came up to me with the polite request that I "just get lost, you don't know anything about it, man." Another boy circled me, wheeling his bike ahead of him, taking up a position six or seven steps away to my right. The third boy said nothing, held his ground, but gripped one of the racquets under his arm. I heard your voice, truly I did, with its "out" and "out," but I didn't think these boys would go quietly, or at all. Not with the timbre of my voice and the narrowness of my shoulders. "Can you get them back for us, mister?" one of the small boys asked, he couldn't have been more than ten, and for some reason that got to me. I moved abruptly towards the taller boy with the racquet under his arm, saying nothing, until I felt a handful of dirt in my face, briefly blinding me, but "I'm alright," I called out, furiously wiping my face. I wound up to release the stone — I had wanted to pitch in high school — and was strangely elated when it struck the nearest boy in his left eye. I saw him fall, saw the blood sudden on his cheek and the others fleeing towards their bikes, the racquets now hastily abandoned, the movement of the bikes slowed by the grass. But this was not to be enough. I bent and wound up again, delivering a much larger stone, which missed its mark, though the boys surely heard it hiss above them, surely followed its trajectory, and must have wondered as they pedaled away from me whether the next one would strike the back of a head or a shoulder blade.

The one boy cried out on the grass, called me mister, said he was sorry, sorry, but I had no time for him. I left him there, his hands over his face, crying, the two younger boys now already retreating across the grass with their racquets. I had one desire only, not an idea in my head really, only one desire, to get back in the car and drive, to tell you, you bastard, to tell you what you had done, what you had meant to me. I saw—how could I not see them?—the sheets draped over the couches and chairs, the bare, unforgiving walls and the lifeless rooms, and I stumbled, numb, across the field, not looking back, hearing still the receding cries of the boy, stumbling forward, until, at last in the car, slumped in the seat—it had all been so sudden, a convulsion really—my face blank and gaunt in the mirror overhead, I said "bastard" and "bastard," and I saw, with a certainty that frightened me, that I'd find you, and you'd tell me, I'd make you tell me, what I wanted to know.

The Visit

The young man shifted uncomfortably. For almost ninety minutes he had sat quietly in the dim light, trying to read the shorter items in his pocket-poets edition of Baudelaire. He checked his watch and thought for a moment that the tall figure striding towards the reception desk might be his poet. But the man before him was older, the face leaner, the shoulders a bit more stooped and narrow. He was as handsome as the poet, or had been, and the brow was every bit as impressive, the trousers as baggy, the hair as wispy and light. He carried under his arm the Sunday *Times* and asked the clerk for his room key with the air of familiarity one associated with the poet, who had stayed at the Gramercy often on his visits to New York, ever since he'd left his American family and moved to the house outside London. The young man briefly considered asking the tall man if he'd seen the poet earlier that morning in the dining room, but he resisted, and instead went up again to the desk clerk.

"You're sure Mr. Lowell hasn't left a message for a Mr. Salkey? It's been more than an hour since we were to meet here, at the front desk. I'm worried. It isn't like him."

"I can assure you there's no message—not for a Salkey. And I've rung his room for you three times now. If they were up there they'd have responded, don't you think so, sir?"

He was as comforting as he could make himself, his irritation with the young man just visible beneath his practiced air of competence and civility. The Gramercy was a venerable hotel, a bit down at the heel, but it was obviously conscious of catering to a clientele accustomed to registering tone and manner. They would overlook the occasional grease spot on the arm of the comfortable wing chair, but they'd not forgive a slight or a treacherous sarcasm on the lips of a desk clerk, who smiled sympathetically at the young man.

"Is there anything more you would like me to do for you, sir? I know it's hard to wait when you don't know for how long you'll be waiting. Perhaps you'd like to go into the dining room for some coffee, while I watch here for Mr. Lowell. Trust me. If he arrives I'll call you at once."

Salkey was not comforted. He was to have breakfasted with the poet at 9, and at 10:30 the poet had not appeared. He had heard stories about the poet, about drugs and alcohol. Of course his poetry was filled with the stuff of madness, of walking perpetually upon the razor's edge, of having his own hand at his throat. It had all seemed to Salkey quite colorful and terrifying when first he read the poetry, and though in recent years, as he'd spent some days with the poet in one place or another, he'd found him less than terrifying, the old alarm now came over him again.

"Do you think," he suddenly asked the clerk, "do you think that we might go up together and knock at Mr. Lowell's door? I don't see why we couldn't do that."

"I'm not really supposed to do that, sir."

"And if I told you I was worried about Mr. Lowell?"

"I don't know what you mean, Mr. Salkey. Have you really got something to be worried about?"

"I don't have to tell you the details of Mr. Lowell's life. You can see that I've been waiting here patiently. And it would be a great relief just to be sure Mr. Lowell is not in his room. That he's not hurt, or sick."

"But don't you think Mr. Lowell would be angry if he were in his room and we were to . . . disturb him?"

"Of course he won't be angry."

Salkey was beginning to feel weary and exasperated, and was visibly relieved when the clerk rang for another person—a young woman with a red velvet ribbon in her hair—to take his place at the desk, and as he came out to the young man, informing the woman that they were going up to room 323, he said only, "You haven't yet told me what you are worried about."

"Mr. Lowell is not always well," the young man said, impatiently, almost in a whisper. "He is not an ordinary man."

"I understand you, Mr. Salkey. At least I think I follow you," said the clerk, who now pressed the gleaming elevator button and stood alertly waiting for the doors to open. As they went up together a moment later, the clerk said, "You have me worried with you, Mr. Salkey. I just hope that nothing terrible has happened."

At room 323 they put their ears to the door and listened. They heard nothing and briefly stepped back. Then Salkey lifted his arm to strike the door, but the clerk said, "No, it is for me to knock, sir. You are not really entitled to be up here." And with that he himself struck the door, timidly at first, then more firmly, eight or ten times in all. They waited, then pressed their ears to the door again. A couple in sweat clothes entered the corridor from room 328 and moved past them towards the elevator. "Is everything alright?" the woman asked. "I think so," said the clerk, who waited for them to step into the elevator before he proposed to Salkey that they enter Mr. Lowell's room.

"I'm not really happy about this, sir, but I guess we have to do it." And with that he took out the pass key and opened the door, calling ahead of him, "Mr. Lowell, are you alright? Mr. Lowell? It's only the desk clerk here, and a friend, sir. . . . Is anyone here?"

The ceiling lights were on, the thick, floor-length drapes closed. As they entered the room their eyes took in the scene with no difficulty. Numerous suitcases were open on the floor, their contents spread wildly over the carpets and beds and chairs. Used bathroom towels were hung carelessly over the back of a dark burgundy sofa. Cigarette butts were sprinkled liberally over every surface. Shards of a shattered drinking glass lay on a counter near the windows. Over the dresses and shorts and underwear spilling from the open suitcases were hundreds upon hundreds of colored pills, their vials and compacts elsewhere in the room. The drains in the bathroom had been stopped, and there too, coloring the white porcelain basin, were the pills, others littering the tile floor under the toilet. Two silk neckties were hung over the showerhead in the tub, and an open briefcase, manila folders just visible, stood against the pale wall next to the toilet.

Neither man said a word as they moved through the wreckage. Only when the clerk sat heavily on a small wooden chair did he say, "Christ. It looks like something awful has happened, don't you think?" Salkey shook his head in grave assent, then suggested they leave at once, lest the Lowells return and find strangers in their room. He doubted for a moment that the Lowells would return, and wondered how long it might take a couple little accustomed to picking up after themselves to reassemble such a room and pack their bags for departure. He was much relieved to be out of there a few moments later and to be taking the stairs down to the lobby with his obviously rattled companion.

Seated once more in the lobby, he was about to write a note to the poet, apologizing for—he supposed—confusing the date or time of their appointment, when the poet and his wife came through the revolving doors into the lobby. Lowell wore a shapeless tweed coat, the wife a well-worn silver fur. The high heels of her smart leather boots ticked neatly on the marble floor at the entranceway, and as they approached the young man he saw the long ash of her cigarette fall lazily onto her cuff. Lowell had his arm vaguely extended, but withdrew it as he ushered his wife ahead of him and said, "Darling, this is Mr. Salkey, whom we've left waiting for— how long has it been, thirty or forty minutes? I'm very sorry."

"It's alright, Cal. I'm just glad to see you're well. I'd begun to wonder." It was all Salkey could do to resist asking him where in hell he'd been, but the poet had no sense of time, obviously, and it was unthinkable to propose to Robert Lowell, in his sixtieth year, that he try harder to honor his appointments and affairs.

The wife—it was "Lady" Caroline, he recalled—smiled dimly at Salkey, offered him a cigarette as she prepared to light another, then pulled open her coat at the neck and suggested they go up. Lowell seemed for a moment to entertain a doubt, but he said only "it's this way to the elevator" and "let's go then, darling." Salkey thought it odd to hear that "darling" on the poet's lips, remembering the earlier wife "gored by the climacteric" of the poet's want, "cycling on her back," the poet "stalled above her like an elephant." But his concern at the moment was all for the room. There was no doubt in his mind: he would not tell them he had already seen the room. That would accomplish nothing. He would allow them to lead him to their charming snake pit as if for the first time. He would betray no hint of discomfort or alarm, would let them exhibit whatever seemed appropriate in his presence. A little diffident, he would hang back. The room would be what they wished to make of it. If nothing—a silent space, in no way unseemly—he would be content to leave it so.

He was, however, surprised when, opening the door to the room, the poet recoiled in horror and called out "my god," as if he had not participated in the disorder he confronted, as if indeed it were not the reflection of a disorder he knew all too well. "I don't think you should see this," he said to the young man, mute and compliant and attentive in the corridor, eyes scrupulously averted, the wife smoking away deliriously at his side, the eyes now covered by dark glasses she had retrieved from the soft leather bag slung across her shoulder. "I hope you have a strong stomach," said Lowell, thinking better of his initial reluctance, and "he can come in, can't he, darling? Though it's really a terrible mess." He placed the emphasis on "mess," as if what spread before them was an unfortunate condition consequent upon their traveling without the sort of domestic help that can always be counted upon to dust and tidy. The young man stood aside for a moment so that the wife could pass before him and perhaps decide at last that the Lowells should tidy up a bit before inviting in their guest. But she marched right in and threw herself on one of the beds, the fur coat still wrapped around her, the dark glasses fixed firmly on her face, the pills and crumpled towels and assorted garments beneath her. "Well, do come in," said Lowell, and "do find yourself a seat," as the wife kicked

the blankets at the foot of the bed onto the floor and silently motioned for
him to sit *there*, at her feet. He sat dutifully, as ordered, and watched Lowell move vaguely about the room, lifting now a nightgown, now a pair of
pants, and helplessly letting them drop again where he'd found them. "It
is awful," said Lowell. "You haven't quite seen anything like it, I suppose."

"No," said Salkey, "I haven't. But really you shouldn't give it another
thought. I'm quite comfortable."

"He's comfortable, darling. He says he's comfortable," said the wife.
"It's not often he's been offered a seat like the one he's got under him now.
Are you sure you wouldn't like a cigarette? No? Well, I'd offer you some-
thing to eat, but there's nothing. As you know. You can see for yourself."

The wife hadn't moved as she uttered these words, hadn't ceased to
stare through her dark glasses at the ceiling, with its lone fixture and its
ominous cracks, long threads extending wavily from one end of the room
to the other. The young man wondered briefly if he oughtn't to offer to remove her boots, but thought she might take it as some sort of statement,
a criticism, perhaps, of her housekeeping. Ha! Here was a housekeeper to
set beside Attila, he thought, though she had, albeit unwittingly, hit upon
the theme that would soon occupy him more than he liked. He was hungry. He was to have breakfasted with Lowell at 9, had left his Long Island
home at 7:30 to get to the Gramercy, and all the while he'd had nothing
to eat. Lowell picked up on it, too, brought out an "Oh my, we were to
have had breakfast this morning, that's right, I remember, though we
couldn't sleep and went out at 8 to get something uptown. You won't have
eaten yet—or did you have something downstairs? No, you would have
waited. I'll phone for you now. What will you have, some toast, some
muffins? I don't know what they have, but I'll phone. Or is it better that
you phone? Yes, you phone. Where *is* the phone? Darling, have you seen
the phone? Have you seen it, Mr. Salkey?"

Lady Caroline—it was not easy for Salkey to name her, to think of her
as anything but the wife—said nothing, remained in place on her bed, the
two men prowling about the large room, feeling beneath the debris, peer-

ing under the beds, Lowell calling out, "You're not lying on it there, are you, darling?," Salkey thinking that perhaps in the earlier mayhem they'd riotously torn it from the wall and tossed it out the window. Perhaps Lowell had stashed it in one of the suitcases, or she'd stuffed it in a pair of his ample jockey shorts. Who knew but that the cord, only three or four hours earlier, had been wrapped ever so tightly around Lady Caroline's throat, or whipped frantically around her ankles as she clicked her sharp heels and danced a mad fandango? There was little the imagination could refuse, given the spectacle of myopic Lowell on all fours, lost in the funhouse, calling to his remote darling about the elusive telephone wanted for the hungry guest. When at last the infernal thing was found, still intact, Lowell was thoroughly out of sorts, and embarrassed, and apologetic, and beginning to feel exasperated with his darling lying before him on her bed of shreds and lumps and pills and patches.

"Look, darling, I've found the thing. I've found it. Wouldn't you like to phone down for Mr. Salkey here and see what they can send up?" No response. "But you're right, I'd decided that Mr. Salkey would order up for himself. Come over, Denis—may I call you Denis? But of course, you already call me Cal, don't you?—come over, then, and just dial the number. You can charge it to my room. Just say it's for Mr. Lowell in room 323—that is our number, isn't it darling?" No response. "Well, then, come, the number is right there, I think. And then we can get to work. That's what we're here for, I think. Though of course it will be hard in here, with the mess. But I think we can do it. You'd best call down while there's still a chance they'll send something."

Salkey sat on the floor and phoned for some blueberry muffins and coffee. He got to his feet and looked around him for a moment when Lowell said, rather more loudly, "Now darling, I think it's time that you took off that coat, it's a bit warm for a fur coat in here, don't you think so, darling?" She turned her head in his direction, dropped the lighted cigarette on the floor next to the bed and reached for a copy of *New York* magazine flattened beneath the lamp on her night table. Lowell moved swiftly to retrieve the cigarette, proposed—mildly, so it seemed to Salkey—that in future the darling deposit her butts in a proper receptacle—"There are ash trays in this room, darling, I know I've seen them, though it will be a damnable nuisance to put hands on them in all this mess, don't you think?"

"If you can find me an ash tray, I'll know what to do with it," said Lady Caroline, and then, "You there, Mr. Salkey, or whatever your name is. You needn't be afraid. I won't bite you. You can damn well come over here and sit down on my bed again. I like you there. It's, you know, comforting, to have a nice young man seated at the foot of one's bed. Don't you think so, Cal? And so well mannered, and, well, pleasant and all. No fuss, no bother. Really a perfect companion, don't you think so, Cal? Come, do sit down, here.... That's it."

With this the poet knew not quite what to do. They had their fun, these two, anyone could see they were wickedly practiced at mixing it up, at thrust and parry and cut and slash and tear. But their Mr. Salkey was not quite the sort of prey the poet would wish to savage. Not when he was their guest, and they had already put him through so much. The embarrassment and the reluctance were written clearly on the poet's face, in his fluttering of hands and his awkward tiptoeing around the room as his wife toyed with the young man. But, truth be told, the poet was also a little amused, eager to see how far his lady would go, how far the young man might be toyed with before he broke or protested or ran. He was, of course, a sweet, probably docile young man, and he had done the poet some service, reviewing his last three volumes and now promising to compile a critical anthology of Lowell's work. One hated to see him done in, but really it was his own damn fault if he let himself be trashed. He was, what, thirty-two or three, and he had some experience of the world. If he wanted to come near the fire, why then let him see that it might well singe a sleeve. And come to it, Lady Caroline was really quite funny and deft when she wasn't staring at the ceiling, even the boy might say as much. Though he looked a bit foolish sitting there with the boots almost in his lap.

"Do you want to come over here, Mr. Salkey, and set up the manuscripts at the little writing table? I can clear it in a minute, and you can let Caroline rest by herself for a while."

"He's not bothering me at all, Cal, really he isn't. You aren't, are you, Mr. Salkey?"

"Actually I think it's time we got to look at the manuscripts, just as Cal says."

"Are you expected home at some particular hour, Mr. Salkey? Is that it? Are you in a hurry now to be done with us?"

"It's not that at all. Really, I'm in no hurry."

"He's already ordered the muffins, darling. He can't be leaving us all that quickly. But I do think he'd like to see the new poems. I promised him a choice—for the anthology, you know. Wants to have someone write about the new poems as well as the old."

"I know all that, Cal. I've paid quite enough attention to know that at least. But he does look at last quite comfortable where he is, and I didn't want him to feel as if he were being passed idly back and forth between us. It's common courtesy, I think, to look after a guest."

With that she rolled over on her side and lifted the toe of her boot towards his face. "Do you like my boots? You've been looking at them for a while now, and it seems fair to suppose you have an opinion."

"I like them, yes," said Salkey. "Are they English boots?"

"What difference would that make to you?" she asked. "Do you know the difference between English boots and Italian, or Moroccan, or American? Don't look at me that way, with your mouth half open. I asked you what you know about boots. If nothing, you can say so. There's no shame in it. Now, is there?"

He looked over at the poet, fumbling with his manuscripts at a small table he had cleared with the back of his hand.

"I think we should look at the poems," Salkey said, rising from the bed. "I'm sure you're welcome to join us, Mrs. Lowell."

"Well, how very nice of you," replied Mrs. Lowell, rolling over on her back and suddenly pulling off her boots. The dark glasses too came off and sailed across the room, striking the near wall, as she announced that she'd had enough of this rubbish and told Cal to just get on with it: "Our Mr. Salkey here has obviously one thing only on his avid little mind."

For a time, Salkey remembered later, it was the last thing she would say, though once or twice she cleared her throat and aggressively shifted the pillows beneath her. He sat with the poet at the little table, rose to let in the room service, and paid the tip with a handful of loose change he withdrew from his pocket. He felt acutely the dread of responding to new poems with Lowell sitting at his elbow and asking him questions. Did he like the Tennysonian echo in these lines? Was his Penelope too severe, too unforgiving? Did the long stanzas mostly obscure or swallow up the less vivid images? Which of his earlier poems did this one resemble? By the third poem the young man was close to exhaustion, and there were perhaps fifteen or twenty more to examine. He looked at the wife lying on her bed, lost in her magazine, or just drifting, and he could almost have wished she would turn on him again, distract them from their work and save him from the poet's steady surveillance.

"Do you ever read the poems to one another, you and Mrs. Lowell?" he asked.

"I don't think so. Have we read my things to one another, darling?"

"Are you talking to me?" she called back weakly.

"Mr. Salkey was wondering. I don't suppose he's heard me read. Have you heard me, Denis?"

"Of course he's heard you, for god's sake. He absolutely worships you, as you know. And I'm sure he'd travel across the earth to hear you keen and stammer."

"I've heard Cal several times, it's true. I don't mind admitting to that."

"Well, of course you don't mind. After all, you are bold and true. He's bold and true, our Mr. Salkey, isn't he, Cal?"

"When exactly did you hear me? Was it at the Guggenheim?"

"I was at the Guggenheim. The time you sat on the floor and let your legs dangle."

"Yes, he'd remember the legs, Cal."

Excitable Women, Damaged Men

"I like to read at these things," said the poet, "though I'm not always up to it. There are better readers, as you know. You can name them. I don't know that they'd be better reading my poems, I wouldn't want quite to suggest that. But I've heard some who are better, more musical, with greater force, less apt to mumble."

"I like John Logan's reading, and Denise Levertov."

"He says he likes John Logan, Cal," Mrs. Lowell said, rolling up her magazine and sitting cross-legged on the bed. "The man is no doubt musical, I suppose, or forceful. Wouldn't mumble."

"Leave the man alone, won't you, darling?" said the poet. "We're about to read a few things aloud."

"I think I'll go take a piss," she said, and disappeared for a while into the bathroom, leaving them suddenly free and awkward and embarrassed with one another. Lowell spread several sheets on the table, handing first one, then another to his guest, seeking his approval, apparently forgetful of the fact that Salkey had thus far read only a few of the poems and could not very well suggest which might best be read aloud. But the poet soon took a few sheets in hand and stood with his back to the wall. He read two poems without pause, read in his characteristically melancholy and deliberate monotone, the voice plaintive, with just the hint of a patrician detachment. Once or twice he looked up, as if to see how far he could go on without having to consult the page before him. Salkey felt himself smile with encouragement, though he suspected that Lowell would not notice one way or the other. When the poet was through Salkey applauded, mildly, and Lowell asked whether his reading had helped, had clarified things. He was aware that the young man had been having some trouble with the new poems, that there were questions he was reluctant to ask. "Quite natural," the poet said, though he'd never thought himself intimidating, never thought of himself as coming on "with an intimidating snarl." Caroline, he said, "my Caroline," had provided "sufficient intimidation," and it was a wonder that she persisted, come to think of it, given the young man's "forbearance." Both noted the darling's return to the

room, her rummaging about in a pile of what looked like silken under-
things, though the young man might have been mistaken, and Lowell
seemed to squint as he moved cautiously in her direction, perhaps not
trusting his dim eye.

Salkey resolved to ignore the lady as well as he could. He had been
moved by the poet's reading, especially by the long poem about Ulysses.
He wished to think of Lowell not as a husband but as a visionary thinker
and historian, one who used the language as though he'd made it. Over
and over he replayed for himself the poet's familiar phrases, wishing he
could forget where he'd heard them, conscious that his own words were
typically serviceable and flat. "The reading clarified a lot for me, Cal," he
said, aware that he'd said not nearly enough, and unsure how to go further.

"What did you learn?" Lowell asked, sitting beside him. "Do you think
it will be easier now to select, from the entire manuscript, the truest poems? I know you've not read most of them yet, but don't you think it might
be easier if you choose and discard as you go? Do you ever do that when
you read a new book?"

"Sometimes I do," said Salkey, "when I review a new book. I try from
the start to differentiate."

"Tell him, then," interrupted Lady Caroline. "Tell him what is the true
note in these new things. He'll want to hear. Explain to him how you can
discard this and approve of that." Her eyes were red, and she stood before
him now with one hand on her hip, the other drumming on the table.
"He's always fishing for a verdict, don't you know? He likes verdicts, Cal
does. Asks for them all the time. Almost anyone will do. Has he never
asked you before?"

"Mr. Salkey has often delivered himself of judgments, darling. You remember I told you of his very thoughtful reviews."

"Oh I'm sure he's thoughtful, our Mr. Salkey. But I'm asking whether
he'd ever been asked, directly, as it were, from out of the poet's very
mouth. It must be something tremendous for him, Cal. Do look at him

there. He's storing up impressions, stories for the grandchildren: the day Mr. Lowell read his poems to me alone and all that. Really quite memorable. Gives me a chill just to think of it."

"Actually I was very moved, Mrs. Lowell," Salkey said, conscious that his dignity required of him a response, some semblance of a quickened pulse, a principled willingness to be, frankly, as earnest as she took him to be. "And I don't mind saying that I'm not likely soon to forget this day."

"You see, Cal? I told you. He's so very nice, and sincere, and he does so appreciate what one does for him. And even when he doesn't quite want to do what one asks of him, you feel, well, he's so decent, as he slithers to avoid doing it."

"I don't know what you're referring to, darling, and I'm sure Mr. Salkey has no idea either. Have I got you wrong, Denis?"

"I can assure Mrs. Lowell that I'm not avoiding anything," said Salkey, watching her sit again on the bed and pull a thin silver bracelet from her arm. "I simply don't always know what she wants of me."

"I'm not always sure about that either, Mr. Salkey. And Cal there probably doesn't often know any better."

"I know perfectly well what women want, darling, and you're not as different as you pretend to be. That's not meant to be unkind. I tell you because it's true, and because you are tormenting Mr. Salkey with accusations he can't answer. I think by now he's had enough of our banter. Am I right, Denis?"

"It has been interesting, I can assure you of that," he said, looking from one to the other, then announcing with a surprising decisiveness that he had in fact heard enough banter, and that he wished to read for them both a short poem, the one he'd most admired among those he'd looked at. "Even without reading the others in *Day By Day*," he pronounced, "I can say with confidence that this will be the most talked-about poem in the book."

"What more can one ask?" said Mrs. Lowell. "If your poem isn't talked about, Cal, it's worthless. Now you're to remember that."

"You know I didn't mean that at all, Mrs. Lowell. Surely even you know that."

"Even I know that?" she shot back. "And what is that supposed to mean?"

"It means exactly what it says," said Salkey. "And you may take it as a compliment, or as whatever you like."

"Caroline knows precisely what you mean, Denis," said the poet, a steadying hand on the young man's shoulder. "And now, before Caroline has anything more to say, you must do as you promised, and read the poem for us. Is it 'Epilogue'?"

"Why yes, that's it," said Salkey.

"He has a taste for endings, does our young man," said Mrs. Lowell. "He's already had a long day."

Salkey stepped to the window, carefully opened the drapery just a bit to let in some light, and—ignoring as best he could the lady, who stood impatiently and forbiddingly with her hand on her hip—began to recite in a sonorous voice the following:

> Those blessed structures, plot and rhyme—
> why are they no help to me now
> I want to make
> something imagined, not recalled?
> I hear the noise of my own voice:
> *The painter's vision is not a lens,*
> *it trembles to caress the light.*
> But sometimes everything I write
> with dim eyes and threadbare art
> seems a snapshot,
> lurid, rapid, garish, grouped,
> heightened from life,
> yet paralyzed by fact.
> All's misalliance.

Yet why not say what happened?
Pray for the grace of accuracy
Vermeer gave to the sun's illumination
stealing like the tide across a map
to his girl solid with yearning.
We are poor passing facts,
warned by that to give
each figure in the photograph
his living name.

When Salkey had finished, he looked up and saw the poet smile at him. He was obviously pleased, and wished to show his gratitude. He said only, "You read well, Mr. Salkey. I envy your students. Doesn't he read well, darling?"

The lady had moved to the window and was already pulling the drapes closed. "Yes, I'd say he does. And I don't mind admitting I am surprised. Should I be, Mr. Salkey?"

"You've not heard me read before, Mrs. Lowell, but I don't believe you think much of academics."

"Perhaps not, Mr. Salkey, though my husband appears to have infinite tolerance for them. Isn't that so, Cal?"

"I'm hardly fond of academics as a class, darling. You know that."

"Mr. Salkey is an academic with a difference, though, isn't he? He's ambitious, is our Mr. Salkey, and he likes poets—living poets. He may not care much for their wives, but he likes the poets."

"I don't like all poets, Mrs. Lowell. I'm very discriminating, in my way. If you knew me better you'd grant me that."

"Why that's precisely what I've been after these hours. I've wanted to get to know you better," she said, stepping firmly toward the young man, taking the manuscript page from his hand and asking him what exactly about the poem he'd just read he liked particularly. "No, you can't look at it again, not yet. Were you perhaps moved—that's a word you'd use, isn't it?—were you moved, I say, by the business about the 'living name'? No, don't try to take the page from me. Just answer nicely now."

"You've put him on the spot, darling. I don't know that it's quite fair to put him on the spot, when he's just read the poem."

"I was of course moved by the poem as a whole," Salkey said. "What I like especially is the line about us as 'poor passing facts,'—I think I've got that right—and also the wonderful subversive question, 'why not say what happened?' Why not, you think, until you remind yourself that it's not so easy as it sounds. To say what really happened. Most accounts go in for cheap theatrics, or settle for a mass of clichés. Sure, why not give every-one his 'living name'? But it takes more than a camera snapshot to do the job. It takes what Cal calls it, a kind of grace."

"A 'grace of accuracy,' Denis. That's it. But you're doing well."

"I'll need the poem in front of me to do better, but Mrs. Lowell doesn't seem eager to let me have it."

"Let him look at it again," said the poet, not looking at his wife, but with a weary, imploring voice. "He'll do better with the poem in front of him."

"I'll give him the thing on one condition," said the lady, holding the sheet before her at arm's length, but pointing it at the window. "On con-dition that he will tell us what he makes of the living image business. Will you do that now?"

"I will if you'll tell me why that particularly should matter to you." Here Salkey raised his voice and twice stabbed the air before him with a pointed finger. "You obviously don't give a damn what I think, about that or any-thing else. And the 'business,' as you call it—you'll forgive me, but I don't believe you care much about the 'business' either."

"I do believe you've upset Mr. Salkey, darling," said the poet.

"Surely Mrs. Lowell won't be surprised to learn that I'm a bit on edge. She's been pushing me for two hours."

"He was doing so well with the poem, don't you think so, darling? And now you've upset him. He doesn't much care for your referring to the words as a 'business.' And I don't think we can blame him, can we?"

"If you are interested in living images, Mr. Salkey," she said, ignoring the poet, "perhaps you can tell us what, in your estimation, makes them 'living.' What prevents the human substance from seeming, as the words say—here, you can take the damn thing, go on, take it—from seeming lurid, garish? Come now, don't be shy. You have before you living substance. For hours now you have been arranging mental snapshots of this substance. You have been preparing to mount and project images. What will make them living images? Yes, take your time, do have a bite of that cold muffin you ordered. Swallow your coffee, that's a nice fellow. But tell me, how have you arranged us for yourself? How would you present us— as living images? Surely the poem has taught you something. No, don't smile, don't really. Just say, clearly, what are the living images you want to make of us here. Forget about Vermeer for a moment. Forget the poem, with its pretty lines. Just tell us—you can do this—tell us about the photos and images you are making with your busy little mind. You won't need a text for that."

The poet had been watching her with what seemed like mild alarm, but did not rise to intervene. Salkey placed the manuscript page on the bed and glared steadily at her as she went on. When she was through, he went right up to her—he hoped she could smell his breath on her face— and asked, mildly, politely, with no hint of menace or effrontery, if she would at all mind his showing her what he had in mind.

"Show me? You want to show me what?"

"Why, simply, dear lady, what I make of you. What I take to be your living image. That's what you've been asking for, I believe."

"Well then do get on with it," she said impatiently, stepping ever so slightly back from him. "And for god's sake don't be so polite."

At this he smiled, slowly put out his arms—he saw her stiffen just for an instant—and took her ever so gently by the shoulders, moving her back deliberately eight or ten steps to the bed. He felt her go limp and compliant in his hands, though it seemed to him that she might at any moment change her mind, perhaps pull away. "Don't be alarmed, Cal," he called gaily over his left shoulder. "Mrs. Lowell wants an arrangement—a living arrangement, actually—and I think I ought to give her one. Don't you think it's the least I can do after all she's done for me today?"

"I don't know if Caroline is prepared for anything physical, actually. Nothing strenuous, I hope."

"She'll do very well, I can assure you. Really, it's the least I can do," he said, pressing her carefully onto the bed, his hands still gently gripping her shoulders. "Now do take off that sweater, if you please," he said pleasantly. "Go on," he ordered, not wishing to frighten her, backing away a step. "I won't bite you."

"He won't bite you, darling," said the poet, allowing himself to be amused. And with that, the lady took off her sweater and smiled pertly— it was not far from a sneer, a curling of the lip—at her Mr. Salkey. Clearly she was more comfortable in her mauve silk tee shirt, the body lithe, the neck gaunt. For a moment he might have thought she looked at him with affection. He appraised her, up and down, with a curatorial air for a moment, then put hands on her again and asked her to lie down. The pillow he threw to the floor, and the blankets. Then he said, "No, that won't do, you'll have to get up," and when she complied, looking over at the poet grinning across the room and adjusting the glasses on his face, Salkey stripped the bed sheets with a violent pull and ordered her down again. He was more confident now, more certain of her. She would play his game for a while. He could see that it amused her. If she was frightened, or embarrassed, she wouldn't let on. That would never do.

"There," he said, standing over her, arms folded before him. "That's the way I want you. Only without all of this clutter. I want you with only a single bulb in the ceiling, without that ridiculous chandelier. I want you alone, with nothing on, of course—no, no, not actually, you needn't cover yourself like that—but the main thing is, alone, not now attractive, on your side, defenseless, like that, exactly, just hold that position, that's how I see you: vulnerable, bitter, exhausted, almost peaceful but with just a trace of unexpended rage. I want you as Lucien Freud would have you— did he have you, I wonder, in quite that way? I seem to remember the portrait, or I heard someone describe it, perhaps not long ago. I want you as

Excitable Women, Damaged Men

Freud had you, or would have had you. I wouldn't want your eyes closed, not that, no, I'd want them open, red-rimmed, quite as they are now, open with fear or revulsion or perhaps a longing for peace so desperate that peace seems almost at hand—the peace of the defeated. That's it. You have the position just right, on your side, the fetal curl, the mouth partly open, the lips raw, the nasal tissue red and a little swollen, just a hint of an opening at the knees, the flesh tones ghastly, the hair matted and un-healthy. Yes, Mrs. Lowell, even fully clothed you'll do. You have made me very happy."

Salkey had reason to be satisfied. Lady Caroline was quiet on her bed, the portrait arranged, her husband's poem all but set aside. The poet him-self was excited, anyone could see that. His color was up. He wanted to learn more about Salkey's acquaintance with Freud, whose work Salkey had seen only once in a London exhibition. The lady seemed to take no offense at the features she'd been assigned, as if she could ask no more than to be pinned and labelled. She did wonder—she asked coyly, with exaggerated politeness—what the photographer, the image-maker, would do with Cal, how he'd arrange that living picture, but the young man was all but spent, and the best he could do was to suggest dressing Lowell up in the uniform of Colonel Shaw, commander of the black battalion in the Civil War. He'd have him stand at the edge of the ditch Lowell had de-scribed in his poem "For The Union Dead." But the poet wasn't much taken with that. He pressed for something more extravagant, while his Caroline, still curled in a fetal position on the bed, recommended that the painter Freud be recalled to service.

"I have it," Salkey interrupted, escorting the poet by the elbow to the ladder-back armchair next to the television set. "Please clasp your hands in your lap, Cal, as you survey the room. That's it, but don't stare so, as if there were something to be discovered. We need a full stare, that's it, a blank, appalled stare. It's the stare, after all, of a man who knows what he's done, what he's made of everything in his domain. You survey this do-main, Cal, not as a field of dreams or a prospect ripe for redemption. You lean forward just a little, that's it, sage almost, erect, as if—with a posture less disciplined by the fear of falling—you might lean further and fall. You see the chaos and the turmoil and you reflect, as with a certain wry dispassion, that you're tired of it all, as everyone else is tired of your disorderliness and thrashing."

"He remembers all the lines, darling. He knows them all, especially the good ones, as well as I do," said the poet, rigid in his seat, trying to be gracious, but looking a little lost now, perhaps not quite sure how long to hold his pose.

"That's it, that's the look," Salkey said, appraising his portrait, "exactly as Freud would know it and want it. He doesn't go in much for mess, not the Lucian Freud I remember, but he'd see it as the true thing here, and he'd want the living picture to include it as well, don't you think?"

The poet agreed, nodding his head, though he was already distracted, adrift, surveying as from afar the scattered emblems of his long delirium. He moved clumsily, apparently not noticing his wife as he brushed past her, as though feeling his way through the ruins, and landed on his bed, where he began silently, deliberately, to pick his nose.

"You might come back from wherever you are, Cal," called Mrs. Lowell, "and complete your afternoon with Mr. Salkey. Or perhaps we could all go to lunch in a little while. Mr. Salkey has just finished his breakfast, but it wasn't much, and I think he's earned a lunch, what with his reading and his arranging. Hasn't he, Cal? I'm talking to you, dear heart, but you don't seem to hear me. What you're doing over there can't be all that interesting—certainly not after the photos Mr. Salkey has just composed for us."

The poet looked up only for a second. "Has he taken photos, darling? I was thinking it was mostly speculation. Anyway I was hoping that Mr. Salkey would corroborate what I've often said—you've heard me say this before, darling—corroborate what I've long believed about nose picking. I don't mean that any one episode is just like another. Do you know what I mean, Mr. Salkey, about the pleasure of picking relentlessly, but slowly, calmly, at tier upon tier of dry snot?"

"I'm not sure I understand what you're asking, Cal."

"He's asking you whether you like sometimes to pick your nose," said Mrs. Lowell. "It's a bit disgusting, but it is what he's after."

"I'm not asking exactly that, darling. I'm asking about a pleasure, really quite rare, that can only be had when you've left the snot to dry out and accumulate. It's got to be stuck properly to the hairs of one's nose, so that it takes some digging and some care to extract it without making your nose bleed. Yesterday I must have hurried it. The nose bled, not very much, but enough to wet the nostrils and spoil my pleasure."

"I still say it's a bit disgusting," said Mrs. Lowell, "and I expect it will be difficult for our young man here to get back to the poems without thinking of you sitting there and examining your snot."

"Perhaps," Salkey said, "perhaps we've had enough of working with the poems for one day. I've already found three very different new poems I can use in the anthology, and I'd be happy to fold up my tent and leave with those—if you're tired, or if you'd like just to have a quiet lunch by yourselves."

"I think your snot has turned off our Mr. Salkey, Cal. Nothing I could say was quite strong enough to turn his delicate little stomach, but your snot has done it."

Not through as yet with his picking and scrutinizing, the poet glanced wanly at Salkey and said softly, "If you want to leave us, and you've seen three poems you can use, I'm content to let you go. But I am still eager to know, Mr. Salkey, about the snot. Caroline says it's not a question to ask, but I've asked it before, and you've been so . . . resilient, up to now."

"He's been resilient because you haven't asked him to have a look at your snot, Cal."

"I have no opinion about it, I'm afraid," said Salkey, suddenly conscious that with these people a line might be passed beyond which nothing conceivable would be forbidden. "I think perhaps for all concerned it might be best if I left the two of you to lunch by yourselves." He rose to put on his coat, placing it instead over his arm, the poet meanwhile picking away stolidly, hunched and probing, the lady rising and coming towards her guest with affected cordiality.

"He's leaving us for our own sweet sake, Cal dear, did you hear the young man? And he has no opinion about your snot. None he'd care to share with the likes of us, at any rate."

"I *would* like to use your bathroom for a minute, Mrs. Lowell, if I may," he said, walking past her and closing the bathroom door behind him before she could grant him her permission. He noticed again the astonishing litter of pills and capsules in the tub, the traces of blood on a towel, the razor blades spilling from a small box at the edge of the sink. It seemed to him that he should be getting out of there as quickly as possible, and he lifted the toilet seat with the toe of his shoe and opened his fly before changing his mind, letting down the seat and sitting heavily down. He relieved himself, then absentmindedly felt for the manila folder just visible in the briefcase standing next to his left foot by the side of the toilet. They would soon be wondering about him, he thought, but he could not resist the impulse to look inside the folder. He discovered two letters Lowell had written to younger friends—he recognized both names, knew that Lowell had included them in his Boston circle some years earlier—and he held them for a while on his lap before deciding that the poet would not remember whether or not he had mailed them. He himself had no particular need for the letters, no sense that they would hold the key to anything. Neither letter had been sealed in its envelope, and as he read them he recognized phrases and postures lifted from the poems in Lowell's "Notebooks." The letters were friendly and confiding while confiding nothing their intended recipients would not already know. Salkey noted that a phrase here and there in each letter reminded him of stray phrases in the few nondescript letters Lowell had sent to him. The "old warrior" was striving still to "pass muster." His critics had been "whittling him down" to a handful of poems. Salkey returned the letters to their unstamped envelopes, deposited them in the inside breast pocket of the sports jacket he'd hung beside him, and carefully replaced the manila folder in the briefcase. When he'd pulled up his trousers and flushed the toilet he rinsed his hands and, without drying them, went out bravely to face his hosts.

He saw at once that the poet remained as he'd last seen him, and that the lady stood precisely where he'd left her on his way to the bathroom. "Everything alright, Mr. Salkey?" she asked, offering him his coat. "No problem, thanks," he replied, taking the coat from her hand, surprised for a moment as she held his wrist.

"But you have been a dear, Mr. Salkey, and you know, I did so like what you made of us in your portraits. Not at all the thing one expects from a young man so careful, so eager to please."

"I'll be in touch again," Salkey said, sharply, "when the anthology is further along and I've some pieces to show you."

"So nice of you to have come," the poet said, rising at last and coming towards him with an extended hand, shouldering aside his Caroline. But Salkey ignored the extended hand and opened the door to room 323. "It was good of you to have me," he said.

In the elevator he found himself rubbing his hands over the rough weave of his coat, as though wanting to rid them of something unclean. He saw again the poet's face, broad, amiable, distracted, the fingers probing at the full, sensitive nose. Outdoors, he was surprised to find that he had walked several blocks without knowing where he was going. He stopped at an old-fashioned coffee shop on Lexington Avenue and asked immediately for a men's room, where he vigorously washed his hands with an oily pink liquid soap dispensed by a crude fixture tenuously affixed to the wall above the sink. He threw water in his face to dispel a vague nausea he'd been trying to suppress for about an hour.

At a small table, seated gratefully by himself, he looked at the manuscripts of the three poems he'd been given, and fought back swellings of rage and disappointment. Oh the poems were good, alright. They were everything he had hoped they'd be. But he no more knew why he was disappointed than he knew why he'd taken the letters. A light snow began to fall on the pavement outside the window, and instinctively he pulled his jacket collar against his throat, though the little shop was comfortably heated. He remembered—how could he not remember—his own long investment in the poet's vision of decline and fall, and he bit his lip with furious self-loathing at the thought of his own failure to absorb and master ugliness in the way of Lowell's famous skunks, jabbing their heads in the garbage cans and refusing—refusing—to scare. He had wanted to come near to the real thing, the true thing in itself, to smell its stink, to look without flinching, eyes a little red and watery, to study its taint on his fingers and taste its foul breath on his tongue. He tried to tell himself that the three poems, his trophies, were ample testimony to an ordeal undergone and mastered, but they seemed to him the token of his own great refusal. With the arrival of his sandwich he rose again to wash his hands, and when he returned to the table with its prim checkered cloth he thought with shame of his earnestness and incomprehension.

Torso

I.

Was it important? It was important. A small thing, sure, but then her son was involved. She would have to tell him that his absent father's failure to send them a lousy six hundred dollars a month was at this point a heavy blow. His friends would wonder—at least they would ask—why he could no longer go with them to the Art Institute on Saturday mornings, and he would have to explain, or make something up. Other children had worse, much worse, to contend with. Of course. But he hadn't even seen his bastard of a father in three years, and who could blame her, after all, for wanting to make that up to him?

She had scheduled two piano lessons that afternoon, and she'd just have time to get to the Art Institute and fill out the withdrawal forms before the offices closed at 6. It would be awkward and embarrassing. She had signed a contract and she had paid a deposit. Jon had taken a place in a small class for which there had been a considerable waiting list. She wouldn't at all blame the director for giving her a hard time. There was nothing he could do, of course. She could no longer pay, and that was that. She would perhaps apologize on behalf of the nameless "other" child whose place Jon had taken. But she would care only for Jon, who had shown some gift for line and color, and who enjoyed the encouragement he got from his instructor.

Torso

The piano lessons went well enough, both children coming in on time, both more or less prepared with their exercises. Jon came in quietly from school at 3:40 while the first lesson was in progress, and a while later she took a brief call from a colleague at the music department asking her to accompany two violin students at their Junior recitals in February. She accepted the invitation, disappointed in herself for feeling grateful, and completed her lessons as planned, in time to go out to the Institute. She felt grimly efficient as she moved from one thing to another, and was glad she hadn't yet told Jon what she planned to do when she left. She blew him a kiss as she went past his bedroom door and saw him speaking into the phone at his desk. She turned off the ceiling light in the foyer, checked to see that Jon's house keys were hung on their customary hook at the door, and slung a handbag over her shoulder.

Outside she hurried to the subway at 103rd Street and Broadway and took the train downtown. Her eyes passed vaguely over the usual assortment of city faces, feeling the arms of strangers seated alongside her in their heavy coats. The faces across from her seemed mostly tired, not nearly as alert as she might have supposed. As often before she thought she would like to draw these faces, though she didn't know how to do a convincing portrait, and Jon often told her to stick to her music. Would most of the people in the subway car respond to her music? They would regard it as having nothing whatever to do with them. The Schubert sonata she'd been working at for seven months would put them to sleep. And was there reason to suppose that other people—people who did not ride the subway—would ever hear her play the Schubert? She hadn't landed a recital all year, and it hardly seemed worth it to fight for a chance to play—what?—perhaps a single movement of the Schubert at a faculty concert in December. As a lowly adjunct, a part-time fill-in and departmental accompanist, she would not be invited to participate in the usual end-of-semester concerts. She would have to ask, perhaps even to fight. And for what? There was no chance that her luck would change at such an evening, and in any case she had begun to doubt that she was much better than some of her advanced piano students, whose technique was already as good as hers. Once she had traveled on the same train downtown and looked forward to daily lessons with her own teacher. Several times she had been recognized by people who had seen her play in trio concerts at the Guggenheim or the 92nd Street Y. Now, as she looked again at the assorted faces, blank or — one or two — quick with expectation, she felt she had already entered a long process of decline.

She hesitated only for a moment as she pressed through the massed bodies moving slowly up the broad pavements on 14th Street. She had thought that perhaps there might yet be a way to finance the art lessons. She would appeal to the Institute for further financial aid. She would phone her sister in Ann Arbor and ask for a modest long-term loan. Jon would wake up at 5 each morning like two of his schoolmates and go out to deliver newspapers in their neighborhood before going off to school. One by one she sped through these alternatives, and instantly she rejected them all. By the time she arrived in front of the stately red-brick Institute building on 12th Street she wondered how she had negotiated the street corners and the traffic. She took the stairs up to the third floor and waited with the receptionist for the program chairman to appear at the counter neatly stacked with brochures and applications.

Instead she found herself shaking hands a few moments later with Jon's instructor. She had spoken with Alfred Victor only once before, at a reception for parents and children the previous June just before the start of summer vacation. He now seemed to her rather more forceful and direct than he had earlier, and she hadn't remembered that he wore his shoulder-length white hair in a pony tail. He was in what was probably a trademark white tee shirt and stonewashed blue jeans. He'd asked her immediately whether there was any problem and whether Jon was with her. She thought first simply to say that Jon was at home and that she had an appointment to see Doretta Swenson, but she thought this would seem unfriendly and evasive. She said that there was a problem, in fact, but that it involved money, and in any case she couldn't bother him with it. He replied that it would be no bother, and persuaded her to speak with him before having her meeting with Doretta. He assured her that he was much more interesting to chat with than Doretta, and turned to fix things with the receptionist before leading her down the long corridor to his office. He led her by the hand, and she laughed at his brusque good nature and his way of reassuring her by repeating, at two or three second intervals, "is this alright?" or simply "this will be better." She thought him funny, but she liked him, even his ponytail, and in any case she wouldn't have known how to resist his solicitous ministrations.

On the way to the office he took her through his cluttered studio, throwing on the lights and asking her if she was familiar with his work. She had seen some of his large charcoal portraits at a group show in the Anne Grey Gallery on Washington Square, and she asked if he was doing more of those, in addition to the somber figure paintings that stood against the walls of his studio. They moved around the periphery of the room, stopping for her questions about this configuration or that person, and he assured her that she had a good eye and asked excellent questions. His speech carried the accent and the flavor of the New York City lower east side streets where he grew up, and his hands gestured almost frantically as he spoke. He offered her a seat on a short-backed metal stool streaked with paint, but she continued to circle, pleased and even excited by his attention. Only once did it occur to her that all of this was preliminary to something else, that before long he would be—she hated the expression—coming on to her, and she would have to tell him that he was much too old for such nonsense, and that in any case she wasn't interested. But she quickly lost the thread of that thought, and asked him further questions about the studio, his attraction to charcoal, and his obvious desire to work with live models at a time when many other artists were averse to working from nature.

It should have come as no surprise, then, that he took the occasion to ask her if she had ever modeled. But she was surprised, for a moment almost offended, hurt, though she knew there was no possible reason to take offense. She was a musician, she told him, a pianist. She had played in a moderately successful trio—perhaps he had heard of it?—and had actually performed on numerous occasions at—well, the point was, she had never really had anything to do with painters and portraits and studios. Her son, Jon, had shown special excitement when she took him to museum exhibitions now and then, and she thought he would like to learn how to paint and draw. But no, really, she had never done any modeling and the thought of it was to her about as alien as anything she had ever imagined.

He held a forefinger to his cheek and tried to look fully absorbed in what she was saying. At once her words seemed to her defensive, unnecessarily elaborate and odd. He had asked for a little and had received — too much. He opened the door to his office and, without a word, motioned her in. The place was a mess. He had to lift a stack of papers from his chair behind the desk before seating himself. The desk was covered with what looked like printed party invitations. She sat in a comfortable, forest green upholstered chair, surrounded by an assortment of sketches: heads, limbs, torsos, hands, haphazardly tacked to stippled corkboard walls. She said she liked his office, its clutter and the unexpected massing, tier upon tier, of images. He lit a cigarette, she opened the door to get some air in the narrow room, and he explained, calmly, that he had asked her about modeling because it so happened that he needed a part-time model, that the hours were flexible, and that the pay was good. She had told him only that she had money problems, and he had seen at once that she would make a terrific model. He would have to train her a bit, of course, but that would be easy. No, he assured her, in spite of the charcoals she'd seen at Anne Grey, he didn't always work with big-breasted models. And in fact her long limbs and chiseled features would represent for him a challenge he had every reason to welcome. She did not naturally exude sensuality — that she knew, of course, he was telling her nothing she didn't know — ,she tended rather to a certain primness, a quaint, even anachronistic fastidiousness. But he would find a way to coax from her features, from her aura of emotional containment, a certain fullness, an openness he couldn't help wanting. And he would — did she follow? was this too abstract? — he would all the same respect her as she was, would not betray her look, her —

for want of a better word he would call it her refinement. Did that appeal to her?

She did not know what to say, so she said, waving the smoke from her face, that she would be embarrassed. Would she have to model without her clothes? Of course she would: she answered the question, laughing, for herself, before he could answer it. And would she need to model with other people around? Again, she answered, of course, she would, and some of them would be young, would be college students, and she didn't know why, but this very fact, that those who looked at her would be young, almost as young as her son, was more disturbing to her than any other thought. But then the whole idea, which had seemed only a few minutes earlier so alien, now seemed no longer alien but rather terrifying. And she could not imagine that she would be a very good model if she had such thoughts, and if she continued to be terrified. Did he agree?

She lifted her eyes and saw his earnest, complacent gaze taking her in, looking into her fresh, sober face. For a moment, as he leaned forward, she withdrew her hand from the table, expecting that he had meant to take it again. He said that if she consented to take off her clothes and sit for him, she would no longer feel so terrified, and that in any case he would very much enjoy recording her terror. Did she think that cruel? She would enjoy dealing with the terror herself, and would enjoy seeing what he made of it. Believe him. It was true. He was never wrong about such things. And besides, she would be well paid, and her problems—well, he didn't know how much money she would need. But perhaps this would help. And it would be—what did people call it?—an experience. Did she feel strong enough to treat herself to an experience?

She was, suddenly, she did not know why, strong enough. She uncrossed her legs and looked down at the carefully manicured fingers clasped anxiously on her lap. For a moment she thought she would say something about the primness business, but what the hell? He was, after all, speaking not of her—he didn't yet know her—but of a look, a type, an image. She was amused, she said, by his deft characterization. Did he always size things up so quickly? It was his specialty, he said. Surely a great gift, she replied.

In a few minutes they shook hands on his proposal and she agreed to come to the studio the following morning at 11. On her way out she took a piece of charcoal from a tin box on his drafting table, folded it into a kleenex and dropped it in her pocket.

II.

She hadn't known what to tell Jon. She could have mentioned, casually, that the oddest thing had happened, and that before she knew it, she had agreed to model for Mr. Victor. The pay would be good, and of course Jon knew how friendly and encouraging Mr. Victor could be. Would Jon have been satisfied with that, or—surely this was more likely—relentlessly inquisitive about the details? They had never talked about the strange phenomenon of the model willingly taking off her clothes and standing compliantly before the attentive eyes of strangers. Perhaps Jon had thought about it himself when the students in his class modeled fully clothed for one another. Perhaps he had wondered what it would be like to sit at his modest table and look up at Ariel Jacobsen standing over him, her jumper and pullover folded neatly on her chair. She remembered that he had been especially interested in one or two fleshy nudes they had examined together at the Met, and once made a joke about not being able to imagine any of Vermeer's ladies without their dresses on. Of course Jon was unusually sly and witty for a boy just turning thirteen, but such remarks did not show that he had thought much about what was really entailed in modeling. And the truth was that she probably made more of it than anyone else would, had an unhealthy fear of exposure that Jon would never suspect. She wished she had told Jon at once about the modeling. Now she would have to tell him not only how it had gone, but why she had been unable to discuss it with him at breakfast. He valued their intimacy, their easy frankness, and he would have reason to be disappointed with her.

She did not fully understand how her session with Alfred Victor had gone. She had found herself almost comfortable in the first couple of hours, until an attractive thirtyish woman arrived and sat chatting with him while he made some sketches and ordered his new model to assume this posture and that. The woman was a painter, a Romy Sinder, with dark eyebrows and a careless elegance that had much to do with her abundant, tied-at-the-waist fuchsia silk shirt, matching Arche sandals and ankle-length denim skirt. Quickly she asked Alfred if she might at some point borrow his model, who was not amused when Alfred said simply "we'll see" and made no mention of his model's opinion on the matter. She was not surprised to hear herself ask whether they were accustomed to talking about a person as if she were not present and not perfectly capable of speaking for herself. They laughed, and it was only then that Alfred introduced his model to his friend and former student. The session had gone on more or less without incident from there, the friends conversing, now and then exchanging comments on the large drawing Alfred was making but saying nothing about the model or her performance. Occasionally Alfred left the drafting table to adjust his model's leg or arm. Once he betrayed a momentary exasperation when she failed to respond to a command, and he finished, after almost four hours of work, by pulling the large page from the drafting tablet and tearing it down the middle. Romy Sinder groaned and complained that he might at least have asked her opinion first. His model asked, mildly, if he often "wasted" a day's work, and he asked her in return whether she thought it a waste of a day to practice a sonata on the piano. He'd already moved to the aluminum sink to wash his hands, and he faced the wall as he told her to clean up and be back at the same time on Tuesday morning. Obviously he was not interested in any answer she might have had to his question.

She had worn her own street clothes at the first sitting, and though she had been a bit uncomfortable when he put his hands on her shoulders or gently lifted her leg over the arm of a chair, she thought she would get used to the touch of his hands and perhaps even feel no urge to resist him when he asked her to take off her clothes. Once, when he held her head in his two hands and turned it now one way, now another, she thought she saw in his face a malevolent pleasure, but she let him turn her as he wished, and almost enjoyed the sensation of resting temporarily in his strong hands. The expected moment when he'd ask her to disrobe never arrived, and she knew herself to be more disappointed than relieved about the hurdle yet to be faced. She had no idea why Romy Sinder had instantly inspired distaste, but she wondered whether it had seemed important to her to have Alfred Victor entirely to herself. He didn't begin to turn her on—of that she was certain. She was no sucker for his tee shirt or his wavy white locks, and she knew better than to confuse lines in a vita with sex appeal. If the amiable Ms. Sinder had gotten to her, that had more to do with an inveterate revulsion to the type than with a model's designing ambitions or lustful cravings.

She had thought, when she was cleaning up, to go directly home from the studio, perhaps to practice the Schubert for an hour or so, then to think about preparing dinner. But instead she called Jon from a phone booth on University Place and postponed their meeting for a while. She walked up Fifth Avenue and considered dropping in on her friend Charlie. He might just be around at that hour, back from morning classes at the Manhattan School of Music and, just possibly, game for an hour or two of duets. She'd never found anyone she enjoyed playing with more than Charlie. It had been several months since they'd last played Schubert's Arpeggione Sonata in her apartment, but she actually preferred his small Steinway to her own rather more robust Yamaha grand, and she quickened her step as she turned east towards Charlie's place on Gramercy Park. She remembered once having heard the long deep lines of his viola reverberating over Twenty-third Street as she walked below his open second-story window, but she doubted the window would be open on so cool an afternoon.

Charlie greeted her as if she had been expected, tossed her jacket on the couch and turned off the CD player. She said nothing about her day with Alfred Victor but told him, vaguely, that she had taken on some extra work. He reported that the piano had been tuned a week earlier and that he'd been having trouble with the new bow he bought in Paris. In five or six minutes they moved to the piano. She told him she'd have to get back to Jon in an hour or so, and when he offered to get her a drink she said she'd rather just play. Charlie rosined his bow while she adjusted the piano bench, and almost at once they were ready to begin. From the first solemn notes she struck on the piano she felt that she had never been away from the Arpeggione, and Charlie's austerely plaintive viola followed her with perfect confidence. In no other work did she find a comparable mutuality, a more bracing and sympathetic interaction. Now and again, as she glanced over at Charlie, square and sturdy in his tweed jacket and richly buffed cordovan loafers, she couldn't help wondering why they responded so well to one another. The exigencies of the music did not much allow her to dwell on the question, on any question, but she couldn't help thinking of the many times she had thought in this way about Charlie. Now and again, when she was not quite up to a passage, and Charlie would smile at her determination to keep going and roll right over her errors, she would think that no one was at once so knowing and so generous. At other moments she would feel betrayed by her own fingers, silently rail at her unspeakable ineptness, and blame Charlie for forgiving her. Was that why, like her, he had no career to speak of? Because he was good-natured and tolerant? Was it the key to his modest success, or at least his popularity, as a teacher, his eagerness to approve and encourage and interact? She found herself wishing he would occasionally feel compelled to stop her, to demand that they take a passage over again. But then she would allow herself to enjoy the music they were making, to feel that Schubert had been served—there and there—and to console herself with the thought that they weren't really bad at all, and that if they practiced together day after day they might do wonders. They wouldn't practice each day, of course, probably wouldn't see one another for another few weeks, or longer. But if they did, she thought, anything might be possible.

When she left the apartment she realized that she hadn't thanked Charlie and that he hadn't asked her to come back again soon. He said that they'd done well, that they always did well together, that most often even his most advanced students didn't know how to read one another. But she'd heard him say as much before, and she was disappointed that there was no further session with Charlie to look forward to. Sometimes, when she had such thoughts, she supposed she loved the man, that she wanted to see his viola hung like a trophy on her bedroom wall. Would he go for it? She thought he might. And would she then trade in her Yamaha for a king-size bed? She remembered that, in a workshop at Juilliard years earlier, she'd thrown a fit when Eileen Fleissler said that the Arpeggione was one extended moan of hopeless longing, the cry of a love that did not know what it wanted or how to get it. She had responded, her voice cracking with anger, that Schubert knew exactly what he wanted, and that in any case there could be nothing hopeless about a longing that expressed itself with the eloquence and assurance of the Arpeggione. Did Ms. Fleissler perhaps not hear the way the instruments spoke to one another? She had felt, when she put her angry question, that nothing could have been more presumptuous, more preposterous, than Ms. Fleissler's philistine reduction of the piece to the status of an extended moan. But the feelings inspired in her by her occasional performances of the piece with Charlie now made her think that what appealed to her in it was precisely the note of hopelessness, of a longing without object or prospect of accommodation.

When she got back to the apartment Jon had already made himself something to eat, and it was not until several days later, when he was about to take the subway to his Saturday morning art class, that she finally told him about the work she had been doing for Alfred Victor. As he put on his jacket and grabbed his leather backpack, Jon said only that she'd have to tell him more about it. He was out the door before she'd had a chance to kiss him good-bye.

III.

She'd never seen so many people assembled in a studio. She'd watched them come in from her chair at the rear. Many were students in their customary uniforms: torn jeans, oversize sweaters, Africana hair ornaments, uncomfortable-looking clogs or rope shoes. A few wore nose rings; others drew with ostentatious casualness on cigarettes. Most of the adults looked like faculty members. They mingled familiarly with the kids and now and then looked like they wanted nothing more than to be one of their own fortunate students. Occasionally she followed the entrance of people—couples usually—who looked like they had no business being there, who may never have witnessed such an event or spent any time in a studio. She stood up furtively and pressed herself against the wall when she thought she recognized two former friends, but she saw quickly that she needn't have worried and almost laughed aloud at her anxiety and her childishness. It occurred to her that no one present would care who she was or how she felt, that she would exist for them much in the way that she existed for Alfred Victor. She would be, she was, a torso, an extended limb, firm discreet breasts, a dark tuft of hair, a straight inexpressive mouth with perhaps a fine fuzz of sweat just above the upper lip that only Alfred would get close enough to see. No one coming in and looking for a seat craned a neck to get a look at her or noticed that she had set herself up as far from the field of action as she could. No one would notice her as she moved along the wall towards the front of the room when the clock above reached 7:15, or remark her going behind the flowered curtain draping the platform at the center of the studio.

A few minutes later she was tempted to peek out as she undressed behind the curtain, but the steady hum of conversation in the room reassured her again that no one cared about her, that they were fully absorbed with one another and would shortly turn their attentions to the art of Alfred Victor, not to her high forehead and puckered nipples. Alfred had told her when she undressed for him three weeks earlier that she would do well to think about her music. If she knew how to meditate, that would be even better, but he doubted that meditation would be for her. He wouldn't tell her not to take any of it personally. She wouldn't listen, after all, and he had seen the way she looked when his friend Romy had visited. Talk about taking things hard. There was no detachment there, no sense of professionalism. Oh he knew it was her first time, and that professionalism was usually a pretense or a crock. But it wasn't as if he'd asked her to pose for the rape of the Sabine women or a particularly nasty portrait of Leda panting beneath the swan. She remembered laughing at all of this as she deposited the last vestiges of her clothing in a carton and sat for Alfred on the cleanly upholstered Edwardian lady's chair he had arranged for her. Very nice, he'd said when she finally leaned back and uncrossed her arms. She hoped he'd skip the comments and the banter when he got down to business tonight. He'd have to know that the people watching him hadn't come to observe him playing head games with his model. She had thought to tell him a week earlier, when she'd first learned about this public session, that she expected him to make no personal or suggestive comments while others were watching. But she couldn't remember whether she had actually said something.

By the time Alfred had taken his applause and pulled back the curtain she was already seated on the ample armchair set at the center of the platform. Briefly she looked out, though she did not scan the room, and noticed that the place was packed to capacity. She was determined not to look down, not to play with her hands or to appear at all inclined to cover anything. Nothing would be so certain to draw interest and attention to her. Nothing would more likely provoke Alfred to admonish her, to address her with that note of exasperation and contempt that could reduce her to rage and self-loathing. She noted that her arms were properly cushioned on the arms of the chair, that her feet were crossed in front of her, her knees bent, her thighs modestly open. Alfred was pacing in front of the platform, explaining that he meant to execute a large drawing, that it would take considerable time—perhaps three hours—and that he would do his best to explain every step he took. He told them about the first time he had ever seen an artist do the same sort of thing forty-odd years earlier, when he was a student, and he said it always made him nervous not only to do the thing himself but just to think of anyone doing it. Actually, he went on, it wasn't done all that often, this sort of public performance, and he himself had done it only three times before. But it had gone well enough, and it seemed to give students a real high, and he thought why not give his students this year that very rush? He'd expect them to be patient, and he would do his best to entertain them by talking. They'd all noticed—those who had studied with him in any case—that he was a compulsive talker, and though he couldn't promise all of the talk would be good, there would be plenty of it. The drawing itself? Well, that would be as good as he could make it, and he would make no apologies for that. For a moment, as he turned abruptly to look back at her, she thought he was going to call on her for confirmation or some witty remark, but all he did was wink at her and turn back to finish his remarks.

When they finally got going he stepped onto the platform to adjust her position. He grasped both ankles and gently swung her legs over the left arm of the chair. Then he stepped back to study what he'd done, and returned to take down the right leg, leaving the left leg raised and positioning her left hand around the supported knee. He told her to extend the right leg, then to drop her right hand casually so the wrist rested lightly just inside her right thigh. He told her that her head was held too high. It looked uncomfortable. She should let the head come down a little and use the chair back for as much support as it could give her in this position. He told the audience that of course there was no superior posture for such a drawing as he intended to execute, that he might well have begun with his model seated exactly as she had been when he had drawn back the curtain. But somehow he didn't find that posture appealing tonight, and he always liked to feel when he was setting to work that he had moved things around, that he had exercised a bit of discretion and control. Oh he was no control freak, he joked, but it was clear to him that if he was going to decide what marks to make on the paper he should also be able to say what he wanted to be looking at for three hours. All this he said as he circled her on the platform, stopping at one point to adjust the studio lamp that hung about a foot above her right shoulder. She listened carefully to what he was saying, thought—not for the first time—that he routinely came out with things that seemed to her ridiculous, though no one else seemed to think them so. She was unable to meditate, or to summon the lines of the Schubert to appear before her, but she felt somewhat calmer than she'd anticipated, and realized that the constant stream of Alfred's chatter—so unlike the silence in which he usually worked when the two of them were alone—would give her something to focus on and make it all much easier. Though of course she couldn't see the drawing, she would try to imagine it taking shape from what he said. She would tell Alfred what she thought of it once the others had gone.

IV.

The first signs of difficulty appeared about an hour into the session. She was alarmed at first to hear him say that it was "wrong," that "even an idiot can see it's wrong," then stunned to hear him ask her—her!—if she had moved her right leg. *Had* she? She was speechless, not quite able to believe that she was being called upon to speak, to add to her public presentation a voice, as though she had not presented, shown, more than enough. She pretended not to hear him, not to understand what he wanted. She would do as he wished, would adopt any posture required, no matter how uncomfortable. But she would not speak. Of this she was certain, though she heard him say "Oh fine, she doesn't speak" and "Will you look at that leg!" She thought that if he stepped onto the platform to move her leg she would be compliant, but that if he abused her in any way she would perhaps kick him or tell him simply to piss off. She would not cry, would not ask him nicely to leave her alone, would not deny that she had moved, when anyone who had been watching knew perfectly well that she had remained as still as he could have wished. She had not the composure to imagine what was going wrong with Alfred's large drawing, but she believed that he would correct the problem and get over his little fit.

And in fact her refusal to speak left him then with no recourse but to return to the drawing with renewed energy. He worked furiously to overcome his difficulties, talking with manic abandon and speculating somewhat incoherently on what had led him to start the drawing with her right leg. This, he suggested, was a peculiar, some would call it a daring, opening, and it was just conceivable that by investing so heavily in that single limb before so much as sketching the figure as a whole he had created an imbalance of forces. He hadn't gone after distortion, he said, and he hadn't yet been able to make the thing look right. Wherever he looked — at the head, at the shoulder, at "those nice little breasts" — he saw that leg, pulling everything after it, drawing everything into its "goddamn filthy orbit." Did they see what he was getting at? *Did* they?

As he repeated the question he stepped back from his easel and tossed the charcoal on the floor. No one responded. She watched him ask a graduate student for an opinion and heard him cry "Christ" when the student mildly offered that the leg wasn't bad at all. She remained perfectly still and compliant when he stepped up on the platform beside her, kneeled down and stroked her calf. It's a good leg, you can see that, he said — or at least that is what she thought she heard. But — and here there was no mistaking his intent — the leg had no business being extended *so* — and he pulled the leg out and down so harshly that she could only stand up, awkwardly, sharply uncoiling from the chair where she had been securely seated. She put her hand on his shoulder to steady herself and in a moment asked him if he would like her to sit down again. The sound of her own faint voice surprised her. And though he commanded her then to speak up, she asked him again quietly, as if her words were for him alone, and took his silent, smiling, hands-on-hips response as answer enough. She sat down again, and watched him return to the drawing, where he labored for fifteen minutes without looking up and without saying a word. When he finally paused and told his audience it was just possible he had salvaged the thing, he asked her to take up her position again — you remember how you were sitting, don't you?—and gave her no grief when she extended her leg quite in the way he had instructed almost two hours earlier.

Throughout the fifteen minutes she thought almost exclusively of Alfred Victor, of the ordeal he had put himself through, of the humiliation he must have felt, not only because the drawing was "wrong" but because he had carried on and even tried to implicate, to blame, his model. Had he any idea how that must have seemed, how weak and vindictive and foolish the others must have considered him? It occurred to her that he did not care about such things, that looking foolish or vindictive was something that occurred only to people like her, probably also to many of those who had come to watch the exhibition, but not, decidedly not, to Alfred Victor. But then she dismissed the idea, thought that it was a mistake to see Alfred or others like him as so entirely set apart from the good grey others who dared not presume or offend. If he seemed unaffected by any thought of what he had revealed, seemed only to care for the picture and for the factors that might hinder or assist its production, well, he would have other regrets later on, would suffer as anyone would who had gone too far, violated a trust. She hated resorting to the language of blame and righteous indignation, but she could not help herself. She could hold her tongue, she could uphold the decorums and go through with the bargain she had struck. She could even be grateful to Alfred Victor for having resisted any temptation in their three weeks together to come on to her or to push too hard the business about her prim demeanor and her unsensuous body, what he had once—only once—called her sexless pout. But she would think of him at least as he deserved, would know him in the terms of violation and—yes, transgression. She did not like Alfred Victor. She took no pleasure in seeing him struggle silently, then noisily, before her, but she did not like him and she would let him know sooner or later *that*. She had been alarmed, frightened, hurt, but she was—she knew herself to be—clearer now, more determined than she had ever been to be equal to what she had set herself.

The evening went somewhat better for a while. She found herself wondering what the onlookers had thought of her, but she wondered without agitation. A few times, without moving her head, she lifted her eyes and found herself considering the relentless gaze of several people. Was she at these very moments inspiring fantasies of possession and violation? Did the bearded fellow with his hands clasped humbly on his lap perhaps in the course of the evening think about taking her left breast in his thirsty mouth? Strangely—she at least thought it strange—the idea seemed to her amusing, and though she knew she could not have entertained the same thought in connection with the young students in the room—they continued to make her uncomfortable whenever she caught them, as it seemed, looking her over—she was suddenly quite adept at dismissing the unpleasant sensations and moving on. Every now and then she heard, as from some distance, Alfred's voice asking her to do this or that, and she responded with what she took to be perfect obedience without losing the thread of her vagrant musings. Only once did the sound of his voice stir her, ever so briefly, to wonder why Alfred himself had not been moved to take her breast in his mouth, to ask her at least whether he might presume. But the thought did not give her pleasure, and she remembered at once that he was a bastard and had no claim upon her imagination. That he did not, could not, deserve.

By ten o'clock, when only a half dozen or so of the hundreds originally in the room had gone home, Alfred Victor declared his drawing a mess and promised to do a better one in the course of a single hour. He told his model to go and take a piss, and didn't turn to look at her when she told him to take one himself. He tore the top sheet from his drawing pad, dropped it next to him on the floor, and looked up at her. Are you ready? he asked. She motioned to him to get on with it. She sat, in her familiar posture, and realized how much she ached, how she could barely turn her neck and later would probably have a hard time bending her right knee. To her surprise, she thought for the first time that it was late, and that Jon would soon wonder why she had not yet come home. If they lived nearer to the university, Jon might even have taken it into his head to come over. She could not have tolerated that. At his appearance she would have fled immediately, without apology or misgiving. But of course Jon would not be there, and with that thought she felt she was prepared for anything Alfred Victor might ask of her.

And in fact she was prepared, felt no reluctance whatever as he directed at her sometimes vague, sometimes contradictory commands, and she caught herself smiling at him as he sat at last, after a little less than an hour, on a three-legged stool running his dark fingers through his hair, looking for all the world like a man who had come through. He had only words of delight and praise for his new creation, and referred with mock horror to the leg he had foundered on in the first drawing. He motioned at the drawing with a careless but eager affection, and seemed entirely oblivious to the fact that others in the room had been sitting in patient attendance on his every move for more than four hours. From behind him she watched his arms move about and heard his silly, proprietary laugh reverberate again and again. She recalled the excitement, the sense of rare privilege she had felt when for the first time he had walked her through his studio and solicited her observations. Now she thought that the works of Alfred Victor she had seen before had never seemed better than competent, and she felt with certainty that nothing he might have done on this evening would be any better. She noticed his tight, shapely little ass shifting amiably on the stool as she lifted herself heavily from the chair. He kept on chattering as she drew the curtain around the platform and proceeded to dress herself.

Tribunal

Was he a new breed? The account manager said he was, and at once he thought himself almost equal to anything. Fearless. Virile. Undistracted by bottom lines. Modest but admirable. He could see it in the faces of colleagues. A man who made a difference. Might make.

Though in truth it had not always been obvious. Not even to him. As a student at Brown he entertained for a while the thought that someone like himself might make a difference. He didn't know what difference that might be, but he expressed a healthy contempt for cynicism and took two elective courses in political ethics. In an American Studies class on the sixties he announced that thirty years earlier he would surely have burned his draft card and marched with the War Resisters League. By the time he graduated it occurred to him that he had taken on the postures of an activist without ever having had to risk a thing.

In recent years he thought of himself as a man without a real vocation. He reminded his friends that he'd been groomed for another life, for another sort of cutting edge. He recalled his college role in an avant-garde theatre production, a satire apparently, in which he smoked a cigar and impersonated a blundering American diplomat on assignment in an unnamed Latin American country. His five-year-old black Toyota convertible—a graduation gift from his parents—still wore the Amnesty International decal he'd affixed to the windshield on the first day he took possession of the vehicle. His kid sister, already writing a doctoral thesis on Hannah Arendt at The New School, routinely expressed astonishment that he hadn't yet burned out on "the money thing" and shifted to something else. Like others who'd known him in earlier days, she was certain that he was intended for something better, something in arts administration perhaps, though he'd never had much patience for artists, or in politics, though he'd never demonstrated a gift for debate or for consensus building. Amused by speculation about his future, he knew better than to believe in new beginnings. If he was destined to be a burnt-out case, he'd face the necessity to retool and reconsider only when there was no help for it. Such deliberations were best undertaken with substantial cash reserves in hand.

For a while Steve had been content with the life of a modestly attractive single man. In an average month he'd bedded two or three new women, mostly secretaries at the firm or the young lawyers who seemed to proliferate on the higher floors of his building like wild berries on an alpine mountainside. When business was good he'd book a suite at the Plaza for a couple of nights and order in lobster and champagne. The ritual appealed to his playmates, he thought, quite as much as it ought to have appealed to him, though often he wondered why he was spending so much money to achieve what was in any case plentifully available in early twenty-first century New York City.

Still, living in a less-than-swank apartment in the East Village, he thought it likely that the spirit of his love fests might well have been diminished had they been set in his own humble dwelling. The prospect of identifying the family pictures on the wall for some earnest young attorney who'd just stepped out of her alligator pumps was an instant turnoff. For transactions of the sort he had in mind—not heartless, to be sure, but at all costs provisional—the high style of a hotel suite was the thing: no telephone calls, thank you, no half-drunk bottles of Snapple or Campari in the fridge, no trail of yesterday's papers or corkboard reminders of appointments to be met.

Now and then one of his young women would enquire as to the domestic arrangements that drove him to a hotel suite. An infirm parent, perhaps? An embarrassing apartment mate? On such occasions he spoke only of wanting to give his lady a special time, though he sensed that this was not what his lady hoped to hear. Once or twice he described himself as an inadequate housekeeper who had stupidly put off hiring someone to clean up after him, but this only led to assurances that, really, the condition of his apartment was of no importance. He thought it best to dispense more or less entirely with references to domestic virtue or incompetence.

Shula, of course, was a different matter. He'd dated her three times in the course of a month, and he was debating whether or not to see her again. A divorced Israeli woman with one child, she ran a thriving export business and looked like she was equal to anything. She moved with a lithe precision, wore short leather skirts and smoked hand-rolled cigarettes, licking away stray pieces of tobacco with the flick of an animal's practiced tongue. She spoke four languages and obviously found Steve Lindsay amusing. Though she'd refused thus far to sleep with him, refusing also his offer of hotel accommodations and a special time, she smartly squeezed his left buttock as they danced together at Birdland one night. Insisting that he show her his apartment, she spent their hours there looking at his old college books and asking him questions about the prints and postcards tacked to the walls. She told him a few things about her former husband and put on fresh lipstick twice on her visits to the bathroom. She laughed at his small jokes and smiled amiably at the nonsense he spoke on the subject of politics. Twice in one evening she reminded him that it wasn't necessary to speak to her about Israel—there were many other subjects she preferred to discuss. A few years earlier, he reflected, he would not have been able to keep his hands off her. Now, in spite of her tight little body and dark inviting eyes, he found her a little hard, a little frightening. He had the sense that he was watched, perhaps even mocked. When she held his hand she might well have been counting his pulse.

He had little to tell her about his business that she did not already know. She appeared, in fact, to know a great many things, and often in her presence he felt younger than he had felt in some time. In the elevator on the way down from her offices he lightly kissed her ear and she expertly brushed his cheek with the back of her hand. Once or twice she surprised him by abruptly terminating an exchange and looking at him as if he were tedious or, frankly, not very bright. When he told her that smoking was an unfortunate addiction and that very few of his friends smoked, she quoted playfully from Italo Svevo's *Confessions of Zeno* and said she preferred Zeno to any well-behaved American she'd ever met. Her four-year-old, she said, knew more about life than most Americans, whose jogging suits and exercise machines represented a fear of reality. The money managers she'd met were single-minded and provincial. The brighter ones had opinions, but they didn't care about anything besides their work—"and not even that, if they tell you the truth." If Steve had time to read and think, then his work wasn't a bad thing. She'd have to know him better before she could be sure.

He'd never met anyone who moved so quickly—not always deftly— from one thought to another, who could seem at one moment intimate and playful, the next sharp and impatient. She had a hunger for thoughts and sensations he didn't imagine he could satisfy. At a Cuban restaurant on 23rd street she interrogated the *maître d'* for ten minutes to learn the name of an odd-looking dish she'd never tried before. She lectured Steve for a half hour on the dangers of failing to have a wart on his palm examined, and she insisted he tell her everything he could about the play he'd liked so much in school, only to pronounce it "absurd" and "infantile" when he was through. He liked the way she stroked the edge of her nostril with a long painted fingernail when she listened, and he enjoyed the sight of her crossing and recrossing her nervous stockinged legs as she went from one cigarette to another. He imagined her the sort of woman who would rake his back with those lethal fingernails in the course of love-making, who would want to draw a little blood if she could.

One afternoon at lunch hour she accompanied him to the midtown camera district. He'd told her about the old Leica his father owned and about his desire to buy just such a camera if he could find one. She knew nothing about cameras, as it happened, but she assured him that she would be a help with the Hasidim who owned most of the shops he'd need to visit. The first three shops they tried had nothing he was after, but the fourth—a third-floor walk-up that looked like an old-fashioned sweatshop and smelled like a damp towel—had just the thing. Shula spoke to the two clerks at the counter in Yiddish, then in English, so Steve would understand. Both clerks were dressed in black gabardine slacks and white dress shirts buttoned up to the throat. She told them they were in a hurry—she seemed always in a hurry—and asked why the shelves behind the counter were empty. "If you have cameras you want to sell, why not show them?" she asked. "You want maybe to sell only to experts who don't need to see what they're buying?" She too was in business, she said, and she'd never heard of selling without showing, letting people look, maybe compare. It was a little stupid, no?

The clerks didn't know quite what to make of her, but it was clear they did not find her funny. Steve tried for a moment to intervene, but she told him it was better if he left it to her—"I know these people," she assured him—and he decided from that point to say nothing unless invited. The Leica was before them at last, on the crude wooden counter, in what appeared to be good condition. Was he sure it was like the one his father had? He was certain. Did he want maybe to try it? He didn't know what she meant by "try it." "You could hold it in your hand at least. See if it feels right." He reminded her that he was not buying a set of golf clubs. "Very funny," she replied. But really, was it possible he would buy an expensive thing, a used one, without trying it? The clerk nearest them, who clearly followed every turn in their exchange, assured her that the Leica was insured against defects for thirty days. He was no more friendly than he had been when they first came in. Steve adjusted the lens setting, tested the shutter release, opened the camera and ran a finger around the cartridge well. Shula said they would soon have to go. Did he want to go further with this?

The clerk, meanwhile, had spread on the counter a neatly printed sheet containing vital information. The Leica had been manufactured in 1954, it had the following capacities, it was valued at $3,000, and it was being sold at $1,850. Did he understand correctly that it was not "the lady" who wished to buy, but her husband? He was not her husband, she assured him. He hadn't thought so, he said, in Yiddish. Her friend didn't look Jewish, and maybe — it was obviously not his business, but he'd say so — maybe her friend was not happy that a woman should talk for him, when it was not her money he would be spending.

It was just the sort of thing Steve had feared, though he'd understood not a word of Shula's last exchange with the looming, repellant clerk. With one decisive gesture his chic Israeli companion had swept the information sheet to the floor, turned on her elegant heels and announced that their excursion was terminated. "She's in a hurry you should leave," the clerk said in English, turning to Steve. "You want maybe she should go alone, and we can talk maybe about a camera?" Steve said, "I'll come back," but Shula told him to go on, stay, "You'll get along very well with this person," and though he protested that it was time also for him to get back to work, she flung a resonant goodbye and was out the door, heels clattering furiously in the corridor, before he could join her.

A bit embarrassed, and not hurting for money, Steve bought the camera and got out of the shop as quickly as he could. He had tried, briefly, to bargain with the clerk, but had given up at once. On his way down the steps, the camera secure in the capacious leather case he had bought for an additional forty dollars, he realized just how relieved he was to be escaping. There had been something offensive about the clerks, something steely and unrelenting. They met his eyes with no trace of deference or sympathy or forgiveness. The clean-shaven one stripped the tape from the carton with a distracted but practiced efficiency. The bearded one, who had insulted Shula, wound his cruel unclean fingers through his long beard with a cold pulling motion, as though he were tightening a knot.

Steve had seen such people before, and had stayed away from them. They were not at all like the Jewish friends he had made at school, or the slick operators who worked several of the trading desks at his office. These two were something else, something that felt old and remote, though both camera salesmen were about his own age and worked ten minutes away from his own Sixth Avenue building. It seemed to him strange, but he could not quite hold them apart from the image in his mind of Shula. Was this a case of contamination by association? He smiled for a moment as he thought of Shula, with her tight leather skirt and sharply painted red lips, being introduced to the prematurely matronly wives of the clerks, blank grey women of the kind he'd glimpsed a couple of times while visiting an acquaintance in Williamsburg. But she belonged with them, he felt, she knew them, as she herself had said, and there was in her an iron will, a resistance to the looser and easier sentiments, that was as remote and forbidding as their efficiencies and their studied refusal of personal warmth or color.

Back at his desk, the Leica locked away in a closet, the phone enquiries and stock quotations all but overwhelming, he couldn't get Shula out of his mind. At a meeting of account managers at 3:30 he drummed his fingers and complained of a headache. Back at his desk an hour later, he answered phone messages and told a bond salesman he was sick and tired of his *schtick*. He thought of dropping in on his parents for dinner, but instead dialed Shula's office. When there was no answer he grabbed his jacket and soon found himself walking downtown. He remembered after a few blocks that he'd left the Leica in the office closet, but that was no matter. He was in no mood for taking pictures.

He reached the camera district and stopped abruptly in front of the grim building where he'd last seen Shula. His mouth was dry as he stepped into the lobby and saw the sign for the 31st Street Camera Exchange, with its ugly block lettering and its graceless black borders. Briefly he considered what he wanted to say to the stolid, unsmiling gentlemen, presumably still standing where he'd left them at the third floor counter. It did not occur to him that by 6:30 they would have gone home to their families. Nor did he know quite what had driven him to return to a place he had left hours earlier with a sentiment bordering on shame and resentment.

Did he intend to demand, or extort, an apology? If so, he was mad. Such persons apologized for nothing. They responded to no demands and acknowledged no claims upon them. And for what, in any case, would he have wanted an apology? If they were coarse, or crude, or belligerent, there were no laws against such behavior, and there was no possibility that anyone could have explained to a Hasidic businessman how he had offended a customer. Nor did Shula come on like a vulnerable waif. She spoke with an air of blunt assertiveness and often seemed to carry a chip on her shoulder. There was no reason that anyone would think her frail or timid. Had she not mocked the Hasids about their empty shelves? Steve didn't quite know what the clerk had said to her in the end, but he could tell from the tone of his voice and the look on Shula's face that the words were in the nature of a taunt. He might then have demanded an accounting. Instead he had let Shula leave, and he had handed over two thousand bucks to her assailant. Not impressive. Not nice. A little stupid, no?

An hour later he was back in his apartment. He took off his shoes, poured himself a cold drink, and phoned Shula.

"Can I see you for a while?"

"It's late."

"Not that late. Have you eaten dinner already?"

"Of course I've eaten dinner, you haven't?"

"I've been walking, and thinking."

"You could come here and meet my family. Maybe then we could take a short walk."

"That sounds good. I'll eat something and come over. What floor is it?"

"It's the fifth floor. 5 G. Where did you walk?"

"Downtown. I thought I would go back to the camera store."

"You wanted to buy that camera?"

"I bought it right after you left."

"So already you wanted to return it?"

"I didn't like the way it felt in my hand."

"This isn't true. You're not telling me."

"Alright, so I did like the way it felt. I'll tell you about it later."

"It could be a good conversation, no?"

"I was expecting a blow-up this afternoon, but I didn't expect you to leave me standing there."

"You could have walked out, no?"

"I didn't know what he said to you. Were you disappointed I didn't leave?"

"You were interested in the camera. I was interested in other things. So, alright, you stayed and I left. Maybe you should have followed me, maybe I should also have stayed. But no, not disappointed. If you expect something, then maybe. If you don't expect it. . . .Eat something, then ring downstairs only once, so you don't wake the boy if he's sleeping."

"I'll be there in forty-five minutes."

The apartment was more spacious than he'd imagined, with handsome prints on the walls and an oil portrait of Shula's father over the couch. There was an oriental rug on the floor—possibly an imitation, Steve couldn't tell the difference—and what looked like a Venetian glass chandelier over the dining room table. There were wooden train cars and children's books scattered about. The largest wall of the living room was covered, floor to ceiling, with books. Shula was still in her work clothes, the child had been put to bed—Steve was taken in for a brief glimpse—and Shula's mother was preparing a pot roast in the kitchen. She had rinsed her hands before greeting him, and he saw that she had long, bright red fingernails and what had once been a very pretty face. She obviously dyed her hair—Steve didn't like dyed hair in older women—and had probably put on fresh makeup just before he arrived. Shula chided her for starting a pot roast so late in the evening, and she promised to come out and join them in the living room in due course. He nibbled on nuts and raisins while Shula mixed him a drink, and he opened and closed the lid of the ebony Baldwin piano as if checking for the usual ivories inside.

"Do you play?" he asked her.

"I played better when I had more time, but I'm pretty good."

"You didn't tell me."

They talked for a while about the apartment, about children's books, about the disturbing Francis Bacon print at the end of the foyer, with its goiterous figures and its mirrors and its couplings. Steve didn't like working to make conversation. He felt more than ever that Shula was watching him, taking his measure. The mother had come in twice, stayed for a few minutes, grown restless, and disappeared. He had wanted to include her but didn't know how. Had she any interest in the grotesque Bacon print, or the piano? Probably she knew not much more about them than he did. Even Shula tonight had little to say, discarding her half-smoked cigarettes like the bits and pieces of the fragmentary exchanges she had no patience to continue. When he suggested they take a walk she said she was tired, and her mother, standing at the door, asked if they wouldn't like to watch the television with her. A special on diplomacy. He declined, and the mother took up a seat next to him on the couch, content clearly to miss what remained of her television special.

"So you're joining us, ma?" Shula asked.

"I thought maybe I'd find out who is this fellow. Does he mind?"

No, he didn't mind at all, though he felt uncomfortable enough, reaching for a sucking candy—perhaps it was a breath mint—in his jacket pocket and trying without drawing attention to put a little more distance between himself and the mother.

Like the daughter, she seemed not to have much small talk in her. He thought to ask her why she decided to leave Israel, or about her work, but he was afraid she'd feel he wasn't really interested. When she asked him what he did, he spoke about it as if it were the last thing he'd expected himself to be doing. Was he planning maybe to devote himself to something else? He hadn't had much time for planning, he replied. It was a difficult business he was in. He spoke of burnout. Did she know that expression? She knew it, yes. She had in fact known it, as he would say, first hand. Shula had told him maybe about her older brother Yaron? She hadn't. Well, his picture was there, in the wooden frame on the table, under the alabaster lamp. He was handsome, no? He was.

"And you know, when he was killed—by accident, in a street incident in Jerusalem—I thought I would make a way to remember him. You know what I'm saying, no?"

He thought he did, though he had no experience like this, he was very sorry, even his four grandparents were alive still, his own parents married young, and even now they liked to dance and play tennis.

"They play tennis?" she asked.

"Yes, they enjoy that."

"And you play with them, maybe?"

"When I can, sometimes on the weekend, on a Saturday morning, in nice weather."

And so he didn't know burnout? Not yet, though he heard about it often enough from people who had worked longer than he had in his business.

"It's a result of sensitivity, maybe, this burnout?" she asked. "The sensitive ones burn out first?"

"Perhaps that was it," he said. He didn't know for certain. And did he think that it was her sensitivity, maybe, that had caused her to feel after two, maybe it was three years of mourning for her son and trying to write the story of his life that she just could not go on with it, that she had to turn her attention to the other living members of her family? He supposed yes, that it was a matter of sensitivity, that she had burned out on the whole thing. It was natural, of that he was sure.

"Natural?" she asked.

"Yes," he said. "I'm sure."

"You mean, by 'natural,' alright, yes? It's alright with you that I burned out? I can be a good person, no? Even if I do not finish writing my son's story?"

He was aware that she had attached to the word "natural" a certain quality of meaning he had not intended, but he was unused to paying to words the kind of attention she paid. And besides, he had not wanted to be involved with the mother at all in this way. It seemed to him odd, disturbing really, that Shula had been sitting there watching without saying a word. Her face was drawn and tired-looking, and she dragged her fingers across her scalp with what seemed like exasperation. Was she offended again? Surely it was not possible that his innocent use of a word could offend them. He had meant only to put the mother at her ease, to say that anyone would burn out who had tried what she had attempted. If Shula didn't like that, she should at once tell him. So he felt, as he found himself saying that the mother should not be hard on herself when everyone knew—Shula would surely agree with him—that it was an impossible thing she had tried to accomplish.

But the mother was not satisfied. So she said, bluntly, though for a moment he thought he saw a faint smile cross her face. Was she enjoying herself a little at his expense? That would be something! Shula, on the other hand, was definitely not enjoying herself. She didn't think—she lifted her voice a little—she didn't think he knew what was impossible, not even what was hard. Here, accusing him, she got up and walked around him a little, lighting a cigarette. There was something implacable in her voice and in her persistent circling movement that made him almost dizzy. He did not like these people. He did not like them, though he could not quite—not yet—tear himself away from them. He wanted to defend himself to them, though he did not understand what he had done or said to offend them, could not grasp how a modest conversation had changed so suddenly into what seemed a confrontation charged with anger. He found himself defending his use of the word "natural," while Shula demanded that he explain what was important and comforting to him about the word.

"Any idiot can be natural," she said. "Natural is an idiot's word for doing what he likes. You think you're talking here with people who are natural?"

He looked at her with mute astonishment. He could not very well say to her what he suddenly thought. That she was mad, her mother not much better. She had invited him, apparently, to insult him. The mother had said she wanted to know him, but was very likely incensed at the thought that a man, possibly uncircumcised, was dating her daughter and visiting her at an improper hour. He didn't like the mother's long red fingernails, the dyed hair only a little grey at the roots. It occurred to him that Shula too might dye her hair, that she was perhaps a redhead, her lustrous black hair a fraud. The chocolates wrapped in silver foil in the cut glass dish on the table looked unappetizing, the foil wrappers dingy and handled. As he reached for one, letting the silence take over for a minute, he wondered what they would say if he let the wrapper drop to the floor after taking the soft, warm chocolate in his mouth. Instead he asked Shula where he should put it, and was surprised when she rose to fetch him an amber ashtray which she placed on the table before him. He licked the chocolate on his teeth, displayed them, and asked, with an air of casual effrontery, whether they would not like him to leave: they must be very tired, he said, what with all the fresh meat they'd had to work at this evening.

"Fresh meat?" the mother asked. "What is this fresh meat?" But Shula said, simply, that he was very funny, that they were all too tired to go on, that she was sorry she could not take a walk, and that she forgot sometimes how little Americans liked to argue. Did he know that in many places it was a sign of respect, even affection, to engage a person in argument? He hadn't heard that, no. And was he not defensive when he was challenged? she asked. He didn't much like to be called an idiot, if that was what she was getting at. Especially not when the stakes were so small.

"You think a word is small?" she asked, the mother now watching with undisguised pleasure, the daughter lighting another cigarette and assuring "my American friend" that words show "how you think and how you are."

"You see a hell of a lot more than I do, I can tell you that," he said, and, "It's been a great pleasure visiting your gracious home. Your son looks very nice."

He shook the mother's hand and walked with Shula to the door. She moved slowly, two small steps ahead of him in stockinged feet, a grey ash dropping lazily from her fist onto the dark carpeted floor. He had been with her for less than two hours, and he felt—he knew—that he would not see her again. She reached to turn on the light by the door, and he saw, as she turned, that the expression on her face was as hard as it had been all evening. The lips were dry and colorless, and she said, quietly, "So you think maybe you are owed an apology?"

"I want nothing from you," he said plainly.

But he did see her again. She had phoned him at the office two weeks later, and he decided not to return her call. A month after that she showed up in person, coming right up to him as he started to put on his coat.

"Waiting long?" he asked.

"Not long. I knew you'd be coming out at 5. You told me you don't like to work late."

They took the elevator together, standing silently shoulder to shoulder. On the sidewalk he looked at her uncertainly. She seemed somber, patient, one hand buried in the pocket of her black raincoat, the other gripping the handle of a weathered briefcase.

"So you'll let me take you for a drink?" she asked.

"I don't want a drink," he said, but she took him by the arm and pulled him alongside of her, around the corner, into a coffee shop with bright travel posters on the wall promising vacation getaways in Venezuela.

"If you think I'm about to take you to Venezuela you're even crazier than I suspected," he snapped, motioning at the posters as they slid into a booth and she took out a cigarette. "And I wish you wouldn't blow that smoke in my face just as we sit down to talk," he said. "I may be stupid, but I know I don't do my best when my eyes are watery and I'm trying to look interested in what you're saying, even though most of my attention is on turning away to avoid the next stream of smoke shot from your quivering little nostrils."

"You're very funny," she said. "You sound angry, like a lover who's hurt. It's hard to believe we haven't even slept together. You're very comfortable trying to insult me, as if we'd known each other for a long time. As if we'd practiced trading blows, and apologizing, and living to hurt each other again. Do you see?"

"What I don't understand is why you want to have anything more to do with me," he said, glancing quickly at the menu and pausing long enough to order each of them a Greek salad and a coffee before going on. "Really, I can't see what more we need with each other. I don't like your mother, she doesn't like me. I'm stupid, or dense, or too goddamn eager to please, or shallow, or whatever. I feel it, you don't have to stop me, no, don't stop me, I know what you think, and your mother. I could read it in your faces that night. I failed my test, I know it, I'm a failure, it's alright. I can live with that a lot better than abuse. I don't like abuse. I don't want condescension. I may be a twerp of a money manager, but I don't deserve to be mocked, not when I can't help who I am and never asked to be admired. I want to be liked, I'll admit that. But I don't need to be admired, as if I were some sort of paragon or something. With you I feel it's always a test. You look at me and look at me—like now, just like now—as if we weren't sitting in some cheap restaurant but at a tribunal, and your people were watching to see if I pass the test."

"What is this test?" she asked him. "I don't know what is this test. So you'll tell me? Then I'll know? And maybe I can tell you it's okay, you passed?"

"Oh now, don't you play that game with me," he said. "It doesn't become you. You, who care so much about words. Who decides what is natural and what is insulting, what is good and what is bad. Don't you suddenly tell me you don't know what is the test you and your lovely mother are in the habit of administering to prospective suitors. Unless maybe they come ready-made with the proper pedigree and all. Then maybe you don't have to give the test at all. Then maybe the applicant doesn't have to show his bona fides. Maybe he gets to pass go and come right to the point. Only the uncircumcised are held in suspicion, right? We don't get to show our stuff right away. Got to stand straight, shoulders back. Got to watch what we say. Mustn't come on all uncouth and everything. Not the idiots, hey? Not the goyim."

He had never heard himself say such things before. He had never known that he thought them. The woman had a strange effect on him. He liked watching her struggle with the desire to blow him away—she knew, clearly, that a few well-aimed words could silence him, send him off with his tail between his legs—he liked the way she resisted the desire without ever yielding an inch. He liked the way she teased him about his "circumcision complex" and casually mentioned that she had never been in the habit of inviting home the men she dated—not for a drink, or a dinner, or a test. He even liked the smoke she forgot not to blow in his face, and enjoyed the way she gave a hard time to their surly waiter, asking him to replace the brown lettuce in her salad and to throw in additional black olives ("You put two olives in a large Greek salad? This you call olives?"). He was afraid of her, he would always be afraid of her. He knew that. He hated the way she talked to him when he was a guest in her house, and he couldn't understand why he was sitting with her in a coffee shop. She refused to say what she wanted with him—the answer was a little obvious, no? She was interested. That was enough. And he? Whether angry or hurt, he too was interested, and it was hopeless—you know, hopeless?—to make her feel she had done him a wrong. As far as she was concerned— this much he never once needed her to explain—she was always right. She had never a thing to apologize for. When she felt like it she might indulge in a few lines of sweet talk. She might show the goyim a little sweetness and light. But as to anything fundamental, well, let those with a bad conscience apologize and explain and make amends. She would no more bend a contrite little knee than her kinsmen in the camera shop.

When they had eaten their salads and drunk their coffee and sparred with each other for more than an hour she invited him to walk her home. The kid would be expecting her by 7:30, she told him, and besides, she could see that her "boyfriend" was tired and needed some time to think. As they walked briskly uptown he thought he had never felt less tired. He was anxious, irritated, struck by the way she held his arm and spoke as if they had all but completed the difficult part of their reconciliation. She asked if, on Saturday, he would join her and the boy on a day trip to the children's museum in Tarrytown. She mentioned a Sunday afternoon trio concert at The New School, and asked when he usually took his vacation. When they stopped for a minute to let her empty a pebble from her shoe, she leaned on him with such confidence that he had to smile at her and was sorry when she resumed her characteristically independent stride. She soon forgot how sensitive she'd made him and referred, casually, to the stupidity of the business types she knew and the "embarrassing" naivete—it must be deliberate, no?—of the liberal communitarians who sat on the board of the co-op she lived in. It was clear that she expected no resistance from him, that they were expected, henceforth, to be as one, that insofar as he learned to associate himself with her views and her confidence he would cease ever to feel stupid and she would regard him as her trusted confidant, alter ego, the goy who'd come in from the cold.

It all seemed to him amazing, funny, appealing. He was inclined to laugh in her face and to make her a marriage proposal, to accompany her and the boy on a harmless trip to Tarrytown and to demand that she spend a night with him at the Plaza. When, a block or two from her apartment, they ran into her former husband carrying an armful of groceries, he was disappointed that she did not introduce him as the successor and heir apparent. The husband seemed amiable, uncomfortable, eager to escape. He asked after his son and promised to pick him up on Friday at 5 for a basketball game at Madison Square Garden which Shula predicted the boy would sleep through. As the husband said his nice to see you and turned with his bags, a large avocado dropped from one and rolled a short way on the sidewalk before Shula retrieved it and stuffed it in his coat pocket. Steve saw himself a bit player in a Woody Allen movie and pronounced himself not at all tired. She suggested he come up and entertain the kid while she helped her mother put dinner on the table. It occurred to him that she might contrive to have him spend the night, and for a moment he thought to stop at a Walgreens on the next corner for a toothbrush. But he let it go and, three minutes later, found himself a happy man when she slipped her tongue between his teeth in the elevator and saw the two of them projected in the surveillance television screen hung from the elevator ceiling.

The mother did not at all seem surprised to see him. She took his coat and asked if he was feeling any better than he did on his previous visit.

Within a few minutes she'd poured him a glass of cranberry juice and explained how, two years earlier, they'd acquired the Francis Bacon print he admired. She got him a book of children's poems to read to the child, and set them up next to one another on the couch. Every now and then he looked over at Shula and wondered what on earth he was getting into, but he liked the smell of the chicken kiev they were preparing and allowed himself to admire Shula's angular features and muscular arms as she tossed the salad and pulled the cork from a bottle of Mouton Cadet.

Just a while earlier he had felt bitter and wounded, but he now felt himself a willing postulant, a witness-in-training of an elite sect whose rules and manners seemed at once forbidding and attractive. The boy called several questions to his mother in a Hebrew Steve could not understand, then turned to the nice man at his side and spoke to him in articulate English sentences. The piano sonata on the countertop kitchen radio sounded remote and tinny, though Shula hummed in accompaniment as she bent to take the bread from the oven. He noticed that the mother had placed a menorah a few inches from the radio and was inserting small yellow candles in preparation for a ritual he'd heard about but never witnessed. It was Chanukah, he recalled, and the lighting of candles was customary all over Jewish New York. He doubted he would be required to participate, but was prepared to do whatever he was asked.

The dinner went well. The child recited the Chanukah blessing beautifully, and Steve was relieved to find that he had neither to recite anything nor to blow out a candle. He intoned amen with the others, asked when it was necessary for a man to wear a yarmulke on his head, and was pleased that the boy wanted to sit next to him at table. He said he'd never felt as far from burnout as he felt at that moment, and he laughed when the mother told him there were black poppy seeds caught between his teeth. Shula spoke of a book she was reading by the philosopher Martha Nussbaum, and asked him what he thought of the idea that every form of love, whatever its object, is always a species of self-love. He said he didn't know, but promised to think about it, when he had some time. The mother said she had tried to read "this Nussbaum," but couldn't do it. Maybe—they could set aside an evening—they would select a book, the three of them, and talk about it together in a few weeks. Shula protested that they hadn't invited the man to dinner only to make him a part of a book club.

By ten o' clock the boy said he was tired, and Steve, seeing there was no chance he would be asked to spend the night, got up to leave. They agreed they would meet again on Saturday morning at 11, and he kissed all three family members at the door. Outside, a little stunned by the evening's developments, he turned up his collar and decided to walk for a while in the crisp December air before hailing a cab. His sense of good fortune puzzled him, and he had an inclination to go back and ask whether some mistake had been made. He was, he would have reminded them, the same fellow they had turned on not six weeks before. He knew himself to be attractive, though hardly irresistible, and by most standards bright. He could tell a story, warm a heart, hold a hand. He had straight teeth, high cheekbones and a repertoire of good moves. But he was not— here he mentally scanned the pages of the *New York Times* "Arts and Leisure" section—definitely not a Vladimir Feltsman or a Pinchas Zuckerman. There was in him something soft, an appetite for comfort and a habit of self-forgiveness. He was tired, it was true, of women who liked him as he was, and he was ready to put himself in the hands of a woman made of sterner stuff. But what she would make of him he did not know, and in any case he feared he would not like this other self any better than he liked what he had seen in these iron-willed people who judged and disposed and shaped and reclaimed with an authority that could seem intimidating. When for a moment he imagined himself poised above Shula, her knees open and inviting, he could see the mother, alert in a black leather armchair beside the bed, calmly calling the shots and keeping score. He was surprised at how amusing, how comforting it all suddenly seemed to him, and he almost giggled at his ability to convert the fearful to the familiar.

A block from Times Square he noticed that a large crowd had formed at the 42nd Street intersection. Reluctantly, he moved closer, felt the edges of the crowd open to take him in. Above them, on a bright, grainy video screen hung from the side of the New York Times building, he saw ghastly images. A bus had been blown to pieces, and assorted limbs and torsos could be seen amidst the wreckage. Helmeted work crews were stepping over the debris, lifting bodies, snapping photos. What looked like an Israeli policeman, a yellow star on his jacket, addressed the news reporters on the scene, but the noise of the traffic and the 42nd Street crowd made it impossible to hear what he was saying. Steve felt himself moving closer, straining to hear, felt the bodies of those around him swell and press against him. He looked up and saw, on the screen, shattered glass, and brightly colored cables, and shoes, and what had been a seat, the remains of a steering column. At his side, six or seven black boys in dark leather jackets told one another to shut up so they could hear what happened, and one of them said it would be a long time till he got on a bus again.

Steve had just made a move to get out of there when a tall, grave, bearded man—a Hasidic Jew, clearly—took him by the elbow, gently, and asked if he was Jewish. "You, I'm asking you, are you Jewish?" Steve did not know what to say. No, he was not Jewish? No, he was one of the shamefully uncircumcised, but with a Jewish girlfriend and the prospect of a new life? He knew, he remembered, that in the past he would have regarded this question as an affront, as a disgusting, parochial assault on his resolutely secular dignity. He would have regarded the person who asked it as unclean, perhaps mad, as fanatics and other devout communicants were mad. But now he could only ask, in return, why that mattered, why "my friend" would ask such a question at such a place—here he looked around for a moment at the ethnically diverse crowd, the sea of many colored faces all around them—and at such a time. Did "my friend" not notice the expressions of concern and sympathy on the faces around them, on all the different kinds of faces?

"Are you a Jew?" the man insisted. "Are you ashamed? Are you afraid?"

"Who are you?" Steve asked him. "What do you want?"

"I want Jews," said the man, pulling him by the arm, starting to open a way for them through the crowd. "Our people want no sympathy, we want no concern, we want you to say what you are and to act accordingly. You know, accordingly?"

He looked hard at the man. He had seen others like him stopping passersby on 47th Street and leading them to sidewalk tables, escorting others into vans with bold Hebrew lettering on their sides. A modest silver hairpin attached the man's skullcap to his dark, curly hair. The others nearby moved back as well as they could to let them pass, but the crowd had grown, the bodies were packed tightly together, and the man had somehow let go of Steve's arm and found himself carried just a bit out of reach. He called to him loudly, over the heads, "So you'll tell me, yes? And you'll come to our table—on the other corner, over there—and sign a pledge card, a pledge, and talk about the bus? Not here, but with our people? You'll come?"

"I'll have to see," Steve called to him, more distant now. "I'll have to see."

"Don't talk to that turkey, man," said a young black woman standing behind him. "That turkey is crazy. I seen him here before, and he's crazy. He's gonna take your money, that what he's here for. You can bet on that."

"You don't understand," he said to her, over his shoulder. "You don't know what these people are."

Their bodies were pressed together now, he felt her against him, and he turned to look at her, at her fine dark skin and coiled dreadlocks and clear eyes, and he could smell the breath on her cold lips as she said, firmly, her hand on his collar, "And you don't know nothin', man."

In Hiding

The movie had left him with a sick feeling. For days he saw, again and again, battered bodies and bloody faces. "Without redeeming merit," Herb repeated to himself, as if the words might release him from the spell of something vile and unclean. At dinner a few nights later he used the same words with his nephew, a professorial fellow with a wild beard and a bright paisley tie.

"With Scorsese, you know, it's not exactly gratuitous violence," he heard the nephew say. "It's not as if it were laid on with no purpose other than to shock."

"Look," he returned, leaning closer to his nephew, a favorite since he babysat for him forty years earlier in his brother's Brooklyn apartment, "I know who Scorsese is, and I know about violence. More than you think. But are you telling me that at the end of the century, after a hundred years of rotten movies, it's some sort of revelation to be informed that in Las Vegas casinos guys cheat and kill? Am I supposed to believe that there is some important revelation about life in a movie that shows exactly what we expect from pimps and sluts and cokeheads? This is your uncle asking you a question. So be professorial and answer."

The nephew laughed. His uncle had challenged him before, and it was obviously a pleasure for him—Herb saw it clearly in his face—to observe that at 62 the man remained formidable. He moved slowly, the result of a knee injury, but he was still a bull of a man, with enormous forearms, an impressive nose and dark, deep-set eyes. His daughter had predicted he would crumble when his wife died just as they were about to retire to the house they'd bought in Delray Beach, but he went right ahead with the move, furnishing the place by himself and inviting all of his favorite nephews and nieces to fly down from New York City to visit him and "soak up some sun." As his favorite uncle's houseguest, Richard could do nothing but rise to the challenge.

"Look, I know what you mean," he said. "And I'm not going to tell you that Scorsese is a world-class genius, a Bergman or something."

"Who said anything about genius?" Herb interrupted. "Who's talking about goddamn geniuses? I'm saying guys like Scorsese are sleazy bums. You wouldn't take him seriously if he was a novelist. You'd say he was a hack. You'd say—these are your words, kid, so you better listen—you'd say he knew how to reach the soft underbelly of the mass audience. You'd come on all severe and condescending, and I'd say, that's my nephew, he's the one with standards. Some bullshit like that. But I'd mean it."

For years they'd enjoyed arguing with each other, at weekend barbecues, and ballgames, and bar mitzvahs. Once they'd travelled together to the Poconos for a gruesome week at a dude ranch and had escaped the mealtime inanities of the other greenhorns by sending their wives off to the dining room without them and taking meals by themselves in a Pancake House down the road. They'd returned hours later still talking, Uncle Herb pleased with his nephew's erudition, young Richard pleased to be his uncle's resident intellectual.

Herb was a little surprised when Richard announced at 10:15 that he was tired and went to bed. To Herb the argument seemed unresolved. Worse, he was bothered still by images that had no right to be in his head. There was a man, a creep, less than human, watching his brother being beaten to death, calling to him, crying Dominick, Dominick, held back, waiting to be beaten himself, waiting to be thrown with his brother into a shallow grave and buried alive. Why should he need to see this again? Why should he hear the man crying Dominick, Dominick, and be moved, moved? He remembered a poem his nephew had read to him one night, a poem by now unclear in its outlines but with a line that had stayed with him: Man is a beast to man. He had said, at the time, that he had known this all his life, but that the fact had never before seemed to him so terrible. Now the thought came to him again, and it was associated for him with the image of those bloodied faces and the voice of the man, a brute, crying Dominick, Dominick, as if he had been tender, feeling, a lover. And he resented it. He resented it and was troubled.

At 11 he took his keys from the basket on the kitchen counter and went out for a walk. It was better to walk in this place at night. The developers had promised that Sunrise Estates would be largely completed by September, but already it was late December, and much of the place was the barren swampland they had promised to reclaim and convert. The ground had not yet been broken for the community center, and only fifty of a projected three hundred housing units had been put up. In the daylight the unsightly mud flats and piles of building materials had stirred him to wonder what ever possessed him to go ahead with the move. His three bedroom attached house was attractive enough, and he liked walking only a few hundred yards to the adjacent golf course each morning and taking his clubs from the locker. He'd met another couple of retired school teachers who talked movies and football, but like him they were stunned by the failure of the developers to meet their obligations. All of them found it depressing to get up in the morning to face the mud and the stalled, silent tractors. From what they'd heard, if new orders did not come in, it would be difficult for the developers to finance further construction. Even basic communal landscaping would be a problem, with houses spread out over hundreds of acres. Herb's house stood on the far edge of the compound, on what was to have been a modest bluff overlooking a gracefully shaped man-made lagoon. But there was no lagoon, and the neatly trimmed bushes and small trees stopped at the edge of Herb's property, thirty feet from his front door. The powerful light affixed to the top of his two-car garage shone onto the vacant building sites looming just beyond his driveway. Only in the dark—he had decided never to turn on the garage light—did the development seem almost appealing, quiet, promising.

Once, in the week before his nephew arrived, Herb had thought he might try to organize his neighbors to sue the developers for breach of contract. He would be more than happy to let them keep the thirty thousand he'd put down, so long as he could get out. But of course the bank would not be ready to let him off so easily, and the developers would probably fight. Worse, his heart really wasn't in it, and his neighbors were astonished when he suggested that those who were miserable could leave their down payments behind and clear out. One woman called him a nutcase, and another said he should keep his mind on the golf and stop worrying about other people. By the next day he thought she was on to something.

He walked slowly over the silly "Venetian" bridge, a narrow cement structure, crossing one of the tiny canals that separated one "settlement" from another. His wife had been charmed by the scale model of the development and liked especially the bridges, with their promise of "something different." Herb had liked the model home, with its high ceilings, white tile floors and ample swimming pool. He had never imagined himself being able to afford such a place on a gym teacher's pension. It had occurred to him that the bridges and the lagoons were offensive, but he had lived in a modest apartment for his entire life, and his wife's enthusiasm had been enough to dispel his misgivings. Now she was gone, and he found himself peering into the darkness, trying to believe that the physical setting was really of no importance, that he would overcome his growing revulsion and adjust.

At the second bridge he stopped and turned on his flashlight, looking down into the shallow water. As before, he was disappointed that below him there was no sound of life, no activity. It seemed to him a sign, a portent, that there should be no life. His nephew had reluctantly agreed with him about this on their walk the night before. He'd said it was a little spooky, to listen and hear no slapping or splashing, to think of the black water as a void, sustaining nothing. They remembered the teeming pond they fished in at Prospect Park in a Brooklyn impossibly remote. "Today you wouldn't go near that pond, not even with a bodyguard," his nephew had said. "Not at night, not on a summer afternoon."

"Funny," Herb had said, "how nothing scared us then."

"Are you scared much in this place, Herb? I mean, being alone, in a new place, where you can't run downstairs for a paper and a bagel?"

"There's a bagel place in the strip mall across the road, a half mile or so. Closes at 7," Herb had said. "But scared? Nah, I'm not scared of anything. I see things I don't like. I'm not happy here, particularly. Of course I lost my wife, and the goddamn mud flats get me down. But what's there to be scared about?"

Alone, at the edge of the development, he watched the cars passing on Okechobee Boulevard. Some weeks earlier he had allowed two neighbors to lead him across the road to a Hooters not a quarter of a mile away. A nightcap is what they'd proposed. At the first sight of the topless waitress who greeted them at the door Herb had said no, thank you, and walked back to the development by himself. He had never thought of himself as a puritan. Always he'd made love with the lights on, and often he'd said that the sight of Sophia Loren's breasts rising and falling in *Two Women* was about as close to an image of perfection as he could imagine. But he had a thing about topless bars, and Esther had said he was more of a puritan than he knew.

The silence was broken by the sound of a car pulling to a stop on the gravel at the edge of the service road. He looked up and saw a tall, mature woman get out and walk towards him. He turned on the flashlight and shone it on the gravel on the chance that she hadn't noticed him and would be startled when she got closer. She wore a low-cut sundress and high heels, and never looked back as the car behind her sped away. Herb thought she smelled like cheap perfume, and watched as she turned into the development and walked purposefully towards the large settlement near the gatehouse. He would no more have greeted her as she passed than asked the topless waitress at Hooters for a date.

His nephew had two more days with him before returning to New York, and Herb found himself wishing he could stay longer. He was glad to move quietly through the house for fear of waking Richard, who was a light sleeper. It was good to have to think about someone else for a change. They had had only one unpleasant moment, he thought, turning out the lights and carrying a glass of juice with him into the bedroom. Richard had asked him about Lisa, and he had told him, simply, that she never phoned or asked to visit. That was alright with him, he said. There was nothing more he could do for her, and there was surely nothing she could do for him.

"You don't write off a daughter so easily," Richard had said. "You wouldn't pretend it was so simple if Esther were around."

"She's not around," Herb had said, "and she'd about had it with Lisa when we prepared to move here. You saw Lisa at the funeral. You know she stayed away from me. More than once I insulted her, and she can't get over it."

"But you can invite her," his nephew had persisted. "You can, in your own way, apologize and be yourself with her the way you are with the rest of us."

"I told you once, Richard, and I'll tell you again. Some things are not to be repaired. Worse than that, some people are not worth the trouble."

"A daughter is not worth the trouble?" Richard's voice was angry and accusing. "You have tallied up your daughter's faults and virtues and concluded that she doesn't measure up?"

"Do me a favor," Herb had said, "and don't mention this one subject again. Understand? If you think about it you'll see that I may have reasons you know nothing about. Nothing. And you will get my meaning when I tell you that nothing more can be said—not to you, not to anybody—about my reasons."

They had said goodnight shortly after that. He recalled the look of hurt and disappointment on his nephew's face, and he thought it remarkable that the following days had gone so well. Lisa hadn't come up, and yet they'd talked about important things. Richard was especially enthralled when Herb told him a few of his recurrent dreams, particularly the old one about himself and his father standing naked before an examining magistrate, whose only question was, "Is there anything wrong?"

"To me, it's a form of entertainment," Herb said, "like going to see a play. Is that me, I ask myself, standing next to my old man? In my adult life I don't think I ever stood naked next to my father. It would have made both of us uncomfortable, don't ask me why, but there it is. At school I moved around the locker rooms with the kids all undressed and horsing around and comparing genitals, and I never felt embarrassed. I never looked away or wished I was somewhere else."

"But that's different," Richard said. "You were younger, maybe less self-conscious, and your father wasn't around."

"Like I told you," Herb repeated, "to me it's entertainment. I don't think it means anything. When it's disturbing, that doesn't say you have a problem."

"Look," Richard said. "Dreams are usually about fears."

"You sound like a goddamn professor again," Herb snapped. "And as to fears, I was never afraid of my father. Never."

"Notice anything special about yourself in the dream?"

"I'm uncomfortable, if that's what you mean," Herb replied. "I've got my hands clasped in front of my genitals, as if I didn't want the judge staring at them. And I can't look at my father."

"Because you're afraid of him."

"Why should I be afraid?" Herb asked. "He's standing there just as confused as I am. I keep wondering whether he'll say let's get the hell out of here, Herbie, something like that. I'm waiting for him to take the lead, as if I was still a kid. Even in the dream I find this a little stupid. I know I'm not a kid, and I should say to my old man: Who is this guy sitting here? He looks like a judge, but he doesn't do anything. But then I remember something and I decide that I can't look at my father or tell him a thing."

"What do you remember?" Richard asked.

"Something is wrong with my old man. In the dream he's holding his hands in front of his genitals, like me. I can see this out of the corner of

my eye. But I remember noticing, when we first came into the room together, that in fact he has no genitals. There's no sign of them at all. He's
naked, but his genitals seem to have been removed. There's a kind of a
closed seam there, as if someone had neatly stitched him up."

"But weren't you terrified to see this?" Richard asked, rising from his
seat and pacing behind his uncle's chair. "Didn't you want to cry out, to
ask him what happened?"

"Funny," said Herb, "it seemed to me almost natural, as if I'd heard
about it before. I guess I knew I was having a dream, and that dreams are
weird. That made me calm. Each time I had the dream I went through
the same thing. Each time I ended up feeling calm."

Suddenly he felt inescapably embarrassed. He noted that Richard was
agitated, pacing nervously and trying to smile at him as if they had been
talking about a small thing. But both were aware that, potentially at least,
they were headed down a path Herb had not intended to follow. Maybe
dreams were a form of entertainment, but the dream of his father was
loaded, and Herb knew it.

"When did you first have this dream, Herb?"

"A long time ago. Twenty-five years maybe."

"And your old man? Did you ever tell him about it?"

"What, are you crazy?" Herb said. "Tell my father about standing
naked in front of a judge? An insult it would have been. And anyway, we
weren't talking much in those days."

"Why weren't you talking? I don't remember that," Richard said, sitting again and leaning across the table.

"You were a kid," Herb said. "I would never have troubled you. The old
man was seeing someone, he was in his glory, and my mother was suffering. She told him to get it out of his system, she didn't mind, and so he
continued, coming home late each night all excited and powerful. Thank
god I was grown up and married. I took him out in the car one day and I
told him to just quit it. After that I refused to see him. It took him three
years to stop with that woman, a real lowlife, and until he stopped I had

nothing to do with him. Esther told me I would accomplish nothing, but who listened? Meanwhile, I had my dream, and I thought to myself more than once, who could make up such a dream?"

"You know," Richard said, "you've been sitting on an unbelievably perfect dream. A psychoanalyst would give anything to have a dream like that to work on."

"A field day," Herb smiled. "He'd have a field day, tell me I'm deep. Maybe he'd want to pay me to be his patient."

They went on in this way for another half hour, until Herb said he'd had enough, and wouldn't blame his nephew for believing the dream a golden key to unlock his every secret fear and desire. "So go on," Herb said, "think about it as much as you want. Write a scholarly article. Cry 'Aha!' every time you think it's all figured out. I still say, fair enough, it's a strange dream, but you can make it say only what you want it to say."

By the time Richard flew back to New York, Herb had briefly resolved to get out more and do something about his occasional fits of depression. He resolved to keep a diary and to become—at his age—a joiner. These seemed to him good ideas, though he had always thought such resolutions infantile and hopeless. Stretched out on the chaise beside the bright blue water of his swimming pool, reading through an ad for a book league forming at the library in Lake Worth, he wondered at the ability of people to do what was supposed to be good for them. The thought of driving to Lake Worth to talk about books with people no brighter or better informed than he was seemed to him ludicrous. Would joining a book club be good for him? Even the question was preposterous. He had never joined a book club because such associations had never appealed to him. He would not now join one in the name of a resolution. The more he thought about it, the more the fits of depression seemed tolerable, fitting even.

Then a letter came from Lisa. Would he send her the security deposit for a loft she'd had her eye on for two years? She needed two months' rent as a security deposit, which came to 5,700 dollars. Apart from that she had little to say. She missed her mother, especially late at night when she was

alone. She wished she didn't have to ask him for money, that she could
say it was a short-term loan. But he knew how it was. How likely was it that
she would be able to meet her monthly obligations and still save 5,700 dollars to repay him? Her job was now, for the first time, more or less secure.
She had no misgiving about signing a three-year lease. If he could wire
the money that would be a big help. Otherwise she might lose the place
to someone else.

Like previous communications from Lisa, this one was blunt. She
learned early, he thought, to come right to the point. Nice of her to put in
a single sentence about missing her mother. A human touch. But there
was no concern for him, no urgency about their getting together. For years
it had all been perfunctory between them. He had a hard time liking her
any more. He had thought she was cold. Now he thought she was an op-
erator, untrustworthy. It wasn't the money, though he'd handed over
plenty in the ten years since she'd graduated from Bard, and he'd told her
more than once that it was time she stopped asking them for help. What
rankled was the frankness of her estrangement, her efficient command of
everything needed to demand and use without any corresponding sense
of obligation or affection. He remembered the old Mel Brooks routine he
used to laugh at, about the 2,000-year old man with all the generations of
children and grandchildren: "And not one of them sends me a New Year's
card." Well, his Lisa sent him an occasional card or letter. But not one of
them made him feel closer to her.

He took the letter with him to the half-built tennis club on the grounds
of the development. He often walked there in mid-afternoon, when he'd
spent too much time alone in the house or by the side of his pool. He
could sit unobserved under the trees not twenty feet from the courts, listening to the mild chatter of the players and the hum of the balls. Now
and then he could look up from his book and watch the figures move up
and back between the cleanly painted white lines. The roasted, chestnut-
brown female flesh suspended on the courtside chaise longues seemed to
him excessive, the squashed or scrawny breasts vaguely repellent. He regarded with distaste the blonde hair budding black at the roots, the lac-

quered toenails and the litter of sun-and-fun magazines. Once he'd stood up to retrieve a stray tennis ball and found himself embroiled in conversation with a woman whose flushed red face and goiterous eyes alarmed him. Today he would not have stood up, not for ten stray tennis balls. He had no interest in his book, but could find no way to begin the letter he hoped to write to Lisa. He had thought to remind her how long it had been since they communicated as father and daughter, but every sentence he rejected sounded like a recrimination. Lisa had no tolerance for blame. She absorbed nothing and regarded apology as weakness. Watching him seated there at the margin of the impeccable grass courts, in spite of their proximity to the vast and looming mud flats, she would have thought him a man very much in his element and with no right to blame or begrudge. How dare he give her a hard time about what was and was not daughterly behavior? Hadn't he always been more of a judge than a father? He had heard the reproach before, and there was no reason for her suddenly to revise her estimate. If he would fork over what she requested, she would be perfectly happy to think of it as guilt money and to use it just as if it had been given out of true love.

"Are you busy?" he heard, looking up at a bronzed and youthful face smiling at him from beneath a white cap. "I saw you sitting here peacefully"—she pointed with her tennis racquet at his leafy niche—"and I thought I'd interrupt you and make you wish you hadn't left your house." He liked her at once. She was perhaps twenty, an animated young woman with clear green eyes and sturdy calves. She lived, it turned out, a few house-lots away from his and was home for the long Christmas break from college. She was a psychology major at Emory in Atlanta, and she was conducting interviews for a year-long project she'd been assigned in the fall. If he was willing to be interviewed, at length, she would find a way to repay him. They could do it in his house or hers, or she could drag a chair next to his and remain with him under the trees.

"I'm not much of a subject," he told her. "I'm kind of boring. Really very simple. My daughter says I see everything in black and white."

"How old's your daughter?" she asked, dragging over a chair. A springy blonde curl hung between her eyes, and her tennis skirt sported a playful fringe.

"She's a lot older than you are," he said. "You caught me trying to write her a letter."

"Can it wait?" she asked.

"Fire away," he said. "I'm an old retired guy with nothing to do but write letters and hit golf balls."

The interview went well. He enjoyed himself with the girl, and told her everything she wanted to know, grateful that she asked nothing about his daughter or his wife. Often he made her laugh. No, he didn't think much of therapists, who went around collecting symptoms the way other people ran after butterflies. Who was it, he asked, who said that one of the worst modern diseases was diagnosis? No, he had never been hypnotized, and would rather spend the afternoon with a proctologist than a psychiatrist. Would he agree that he was a bit of a narcissist? Only if she told him she'd never met anyone so intelligent and interesting. He expected, he said, to read the results of her research before they were handed in: "That way," he went on, "I can point out the places in the report that are too sophisticated for a psychology professor." He wondered at his own volubility and instinct for mischief. When she left him, seated still under the trees, he played back their session and smiled at what he took to be surprising expressions of wit and gaiety.

In the evening he phoned Lisa and left a message on her machine. "This is your father," he said, "and I want you to know that you are welcome to the money, though there is not much to spare. I attach one condition. I expect you to visit me this spring for at least a few days, and will send you a ticket as soon as you give me the dates. Meanwhile, my bank down here will wire the money to the account number you kindly provided. I hope that expression, 'kindly provided,' will make you laugh. I want us to laugh together again. Fair enough? Anyway, have a good night, and let me know that the money arrived safely."

But Lisa didn't call. He phoned the bank to be sure the transfer had gone through and learned that Lisa had withdrawn the money the day after it was deposited in her account. After two weeks he was angry enough to call her again, but the phone had been disconnected, and her new number was unlisted. Of course she was busy, he reasoned, with moving and banks and telephone companies. But not to give him her number or address! He didn't even know where she worked, and she changed friends so quickly he could never keep track, even in the old days. He phoned Richard, who sounded embarrassed when asked if he knew how to get in touch with Lisa. "Good, you're making contact," he said. "Good my ass," Herb returned. "I sent her money for a new place and she doesn't send me her number or address. An edifying tale, no?" He hated the mingled rage and self-pity in his voice, and wondered at his inexhaustible capacity to let his daughter humiliate him.

One night he went to a residents' meeting in an ugly pre-fab structure thrown up in two days to hold large gatherings. Bare walls, bright track lights, plastic folding chairs. The mood was peculiar. Lamentation and threat alternated with hilarity and displays of good fellowship. Some women were dressed as if they were soon to go dancing at a nightclub. Others wore sweatsuits or lurid nylon parkas. One elderly woman announced she was about to throw up, and would do so "if the gentleman with the ugly cigar doesn't put it out." Herb took notes and thought of a satirical sketch he would try to write. If he knew where the hell Lisa was he'd send it to her. He was surprised—this he'd surely have told Lisa— that he had nothing to say to his neighbors. Every time they opened their mouths he shut his eyes. So much annoyance, so much mirth, so little grasp. That is what he thought. So little sense that they'd been here before, said the same things, laughed at the same inanities. All that really mattered, he thought, was that those who couldn't afford to leave would have to live with the mud and the complaints. Things were never what they were supposed to be. But they weren't always intolerable either. The houses themselves were fine. The pool waters were soothing, the golf courses green. There was no snow to shovel or subway pickpockets to look out for. Those who were, all the same, unhappy, could walk the few hundred yards up the road and stare at the naked breasts in Hooters. Ingratitude, he wanted to proclaim to his neighbors. "Ingratitude makes everything dim and disappointing." But he continued to take notes and keep his thoughts to himself.

He walked back to his house with the young psychology major, who had three days left to her winter vacation. She had gone to the meeting, she said, in hopes of seeing him. She expected he'd have mischievous things to say. Her parents, she informed him, were away at a convention in Tampa, and the house had begun to seem very quiet. "So quiet," she said, "that sometimes I come out here at night just to see if I can hear a frog or a cricket." They stopped on one of the bridges and laughed into the enveloping quiet.

"Come over to my place for a nightcap?" he asked.

"Why not?" she replied. "If you'll show me what you were writing back there."

But he didn't show her. Instead he took her through the house and talked a little about a few of the pictures on the wall.

"Which one is your daughter?" she asked.

"I haven't put up a picture of Lisa," he said. "Reminds me of how pissed I get when she's around."

"But you write her letters," she said.

"And send her money. And leave her phone messages she doesn't answer."

"You need counselling," she suddenly announced. "You need someone to talk with you about Lisa."

"That's a funny idea," he said, surprised, "that you think counselling is an answer. How do you know there's an answer if you don't really know there's a problem?"

"You're very defensive," she said. "Did anyone ever tell you that?"

"Come over here," he said. "Don't sit there. Get up and follow me." He led her to a battered desk in the large master bedroom and retrieved from the bottom drawer a tattered photograph album. "Now sit down," he ordered, directing her to the edge of the bed. "I want to show you some pictures of a man who is not defensive. A quarterback, a coach, a doer. An ass-kicker when he had to be."

She studied the pictures as he pointed at them and told their stories. She giggled at the jock poses and the clippings of state finals and county championships.

"What's funny?" he asked.

"You're funny," she said, "and defensive."

Back at the kitchen table, she stared at him over a bottle of chianti and insisted he tell her about Lisa, and after resisting her for a while he was exhausted and could resist her no further.

"Believe me," he said. "Lisa can take care of herself."

"That's why she asks you for help?"

"She asks because I give, not because she needs. That you can't be expected to see. And anyway, why the hell am I telling you this? Can you tell me that?"

"I can see," she said, ignoring his question, "that something happened and you won't forget it."

"Look," he said. "If I told you it wouldn't change a thing."

"Do I insult you when I say I'd like to help? That I'd like to know you better so I can help?" She had assumed what seemed to him an especially soothing tone. Did they teach them this? he wondered. In a class?

"Well, that depends," he said. "If I want to be insulted, I can be insulted. If I want to think you're a lot older than you are, then hell, I can let you play therapist at my expense and watch you find out the truth about the helping professions. That they don't help."

"Will you tell me what Lisa did to hurt your feelings?" she persisted.

"She didn't hurt my feelings. Shit. You really want to hear this, don't you? Lisa hurt herself. She got me to pay for three goddamn abortions in two years. And she enjoyed letting me know she didn't give a good goddamn about the fathers or the fetuses. That's the long and the short of it, sweetie. I don't like her and I don't like the pain she gives me. It's not complicated and it's not neurotic. I'm a man of a certain age and I've got a right to be disgusted. Or do they teach you something else in counselling school?"

"I don't go to counselling school, Herb, and you know it. But I'm honored that you told me about Lisa."

"You're honored?" he almost shouted. "What's the honor? An old man tells you his daughter is a predator and a lowlife, and you're honored?"

"You're not an old man, Herb. You're younger than you think."

"Oh I get it," he said, trying to seem amused. "You're honored and I'm young. That's pretty strange, no? Some would say miraculous."

"You can't turn everything into a joke, Herb," she said, briefly stroking the back of his hand, which rested limply on the table in front of her. "And you can't keep everything to yourself. Am I right? That you don't tell anyone what you're thinking?"

"Sometimes I tell," he said weakly, "but not often, that much is true." He lifted his hand and used it to support his chin.

"And why me, Herb? If you don't talk to the people you love—probably not even the nephew you told me about—why me?"

"Maybe you're better-looking than my nephew. Maybe I'm just very tired tonight and can't resist you when you pressure me. There might be a hundred reasons. Maybe I just want to confront you with the idea that sometimes nothing can be done. Remember, I'm a teacher. I'm big on the teaching mission. I want to get through to you as much as you want to get through to me. Don't ask me why. And so I say to you, as bluntly as I can, Lisa is what she is, you're what you are, and at sixty-two I'm an old man."

"Let's get back to your first reason, Herb," she said, pointing back over her shoulder. "That's not the reason of an old man."

"I'm lucky you don't bring me up on charges," he smiled. "Turn me in at the security booth for soliciting coeds."

But she didn't turn him in, and he didn't invite her or allow her to spend the night, though he had an idea she'd have accepted. Young girls with sturdy calves and high cheekbones had no business hanging out late at night with men who could be their grandfathers. They had no business drinking out of the old boy's glass when they'd finished with their own.

He ran his tongue over the rim of her glass and imagined he tasted her through the sickly-sweet residue of the chianti. He'd wanted to walk her back, but he was afraid she'd offer to kiss him, or worse, invite him in. And he'd hate himself, and fear more than anything her leading him to her parents' room. His heart raced as he thought of that broad, inviting expanse of comforter and feather pillows, of her small awkward face and practised limbs, her sense that there was nothing she could not accomplish if she tried. He had wanted to thank her for putting up with him, but he had said only that, next day, she would find him, if she liked, under the trees by the tennis courts. Early or late. He'd be hiding out in the usual place.

The French Lesson

I.

A life. In Paris. With friends. It's what she'd wanted. For a time it had seemed she was capable of wanting nothing else. The move, from picture-book fantasies and sepia-souvenir postcards to loan-a-home and international exchange inquiries, was sudden, the result of what felt like a seizure of purpose, a recoil of disgust from everything that had been her life. She was young, had tried very little, tasted few of the pleasures others had recommended. She had been, briefly, in love, had travelled, once or twice, in a first-class compartment, had stayed for three nights at the St. Moritz on Central Park in what was to have been a memorable long weekend in New York. A few evenings she'd spent at dinner tables across from interesting people—later she remembered only the awkward silences when she'd been unable to parry or return a mild but obviously testing thrust. At school she'd done well enough, had written at Penn a competent senior thesis on women and war. Friends complimented her on her taste in clothing. The occasional men in her life thought her especially attractive in the dark blazers and woollen slacks she wore most days to work. She was earnest, friendly, observant of decorums, reluctant to take offense. No one ever told her she was a bore. When she decided to leave everything behind, she could only wonder at how little it all meant to her.

Of course she'd read about Paris a little, seen the obligatory films and tacked to the walls of her tiny college dorm room the familiar Doisneau black and whites. She was determined to resist triteness and deception and had read enough about the manufacture of images to smile now and then at her own ripe susceptibility. Only once when she was still new to the independent working life she led in New York had she allowed herself to think about getting away. Later, when she imagined more frequently a life elsewhere, she found herself drawn now to London, now to Rome— though she spoke no Italian—but only very occasionally to Paris, which seemed somehow too appealing to seem fully plausible. When she wanted to think of reasons to resist Paris, she had only to recall the stories she'd heard about ethnic strife and articles she'd read about French anti-semitism.

Had they been asked, not one of her close friends in New York would have remembered her saying anything about Paris. She believed—or at least pretended to believe—that usually people went to live in other countries because they weren't good at living well where they were born. They were no more likely to make a go of it in Paris or London than in New York.

She first entertained the thought of Paris seriously when her friend Daniel announced one evening at a Brasserie on the East Side that he'd been assigned to the French offices of Fairchild Publications for not less than three years. She would miss him, she told him, and for an hour or so she actually thought she would. They were reliable friends, after all. They worked in the same downtown office building, had quick lunches together once or twice each week, and occasionally went out for dinner or a movie, though they'd never so much as held hands or talked about the fact that neither seemed to have much aptitude for flirtation or, indeed, much in the way of sexual appetite. Daniel declared himself the least likely journalist ever to represent Fairchild in Paris, and though she declared him, *au contraire*, in every way a suitable novice and a quick learner, she secretly thought him as unlikely a candidate as herself. When she'd finished saying, and thinking, how much she'd miss him, and promised to bring to the office a good French grammar she'd kept from college, she allowed herself to wonder aloud whether it might not be possible for her to visit him in August, when she had three weeks' vacation. Neither of them knew that most Parisians leave the city in August, and that tourists then found much of the city a little dim. But that was a small matter. When she traveled to Paris, at last, she went not for three weeks but for an indefinite period, and she left not in August but in June. Daniel, who had by that time failed to answer any of her recent letters, was in the end of no consequence in her plans, and if she hoped at all to find in Paris a man, he would if at all possible resemble Daniel very little. In fact, he would resemble no one she had known, for if he did, she would have nothing to do with him.

She began looking at vacation brochures a week after her twenty-fifth birthday, in April of 1973. Daniel had been gone for several months, and though his letters had been sparse and sometimes perfunctory, they did assure her that Paris offered certain opportunities that women like herself might conceivably pursue. When she compared the Parisian prospect with all that was available to her in New York, she was struck by her own, almost total failure to make of her present life a rich and various thing. She wondered why she had never been to dinner in Chinatown, never been anything but revolted by the sleaze and lights of midtown, passed up a subscription to City Ballet's Stravinsky Festival. Would she be more responsive to the barrage of sensory delights Paris offered? She vowed to open herself more generously to New York, to see if she could not make herself worthy of Paris.

For some weeks, just at that time, she had been seeing a man two years younger, and considerably shorter, than she. He called himself her "little man," and though she told him more than once that it made her uncomfortable, she liked him and liked especially his neatly appointed limbs and cool avidity. He was already a successful money manager at the Swiss Bank, and though he often worked long hours, he invited her to late night suppers and occasionally took her dancing at a noisy Latino club on Columbus Avenue. Though she spoke no Spanish and understood only a few words, she warmed at once to the hot rhythms of mambo and samba and hardly noticed the closeness and smoke and sweaty stench of the place. Her little man seemed to have eyes only for her, and he moved so adeptly and unself-consciously among the loose bodies that she almost thought him handsome. The attraction was short-lived. Mostly she resisted his efforts to lure her back to his apartment, and though she did once invite him back to hers, she found that he was no Latin lover and that his small smooth limbs were far and away his most impressive feature. Of course she told him nothing about Paris.

In fact, none of the men she met during her final year in New York inspired confidence. The magazines she read were full of cautionary tales about women who lived only for their men and felt they were nothing without them. These articles seemed to her important, and she remembered how in college she had been stirred by *The Second Sex* and promised herself a life built to gratify her own desires. But that resolve was already a little beside the point. For some time she had seemed to herself to resemble the woman she'd promised not to become.

Almost at once Paris moved her to a first new resolve. She enrolled in a saturation language program that met five nights each week at the New School on 12th Street in the Village. She hurried to the 6 p.m. classes from work each weeknight, grabbing a sandwich or a limp hot plate at the New School cafeteria in the basement before taking the elevator to her fourth-floor classroom. One night they conducted their class in a makeshift gallery on the third floor where the Buchenwald cart paintings of Rico Lebrun were displayed. The students did their best to discuss the merits of the geometrically complex, symbolically loaded paintings. The instructor did his best to intervene at strategic moments to demand clarification. He asked her more than once to speak more loudly, to say more precisely what she saw in the work she was looking at. She wondered every now and then what all of this had to do with her life, with her hunger for change, with Paris. Then she remembered why she was putting herself through what often seemed a pain and a humiliation. She had little use for the paintings, with their twisted limbs and carefully organized surfaces. But she was pleased with her own growing fluency, and only a little surprised when she heard herself accepting—in French—her instructor's invitation to have a drink with him after class.

The instructor, a Monsieur LeSaux, had lived in New York for almost twenty years, though he summered in Nice, where he'd gone to school as a boy and still had many friends. He was amiable, or as amiable as he could be given his refusal to let her utter so much as a phrase to him in English. This she found amusing and preposterous. She went along with it on the grounds that their time together would be good for her, though she resented his capacity to speak comfortably to her when she had to struggle for every sentence she meant to say. Had she been up to it she might well have reflected on the relationship of power he had contrived for her, a relationship in which she would necessarily submit to a principled imperative because it was good for her and he would enjoy the control he exercised because she submitted willingly. As it was she managed at least to ask him if he enjoyed prolonging her obvious discomfort, and he could reply only that she seemed to him perfectly comfortable, though comfort itself was perhaps too highly prized by Americans of her generation. In this way they went on for more than two hours, only briefly moving beyond the mildly pointed banter in which he seemed quite practiced. If she wished to bring the encounter to an end she gave no such indication, and he could only have assumed that she was flattered by his persistent inquisition.

Later, when she walked uptown to her apartment—she refused to let Monsieur LeSaux put her in a taxi—she permitted herself more fully to acknowledge a grievance she'd never register. Had he taken advantage of her? There were those who would think so, others who would remind her that she was a big girl and fully equipped to say no to conditions dictated to her by men. Of course she also had to admit to herself that Monsieur LeSaux was preternaturally good-looking, if also long in the tooth for a suitor. At fifty—he might even have been sixty—he moved with admirable athleticism and grace. Seated across from him she had been acutely aware of a painful disparity in experience and authority that had nothing to do with his being her teacher or with her still primitive French.

That he was, all the same, a modest man was conveyed in the ease and familiarity of his conversation. So far as she could tell, he had nothing he cared to hide. She understood him to say that he had counted on an academic career which, unfortunately, had eluded him. He taught intermediate French in the evening division at the New School because he needed work and otherwise relied on this and that to survive. Why had he stayed in New York? He could not say, beyond the fact that a return to France was now unthinkable.

When she saw him again on Monday of the following week she found herself vaguely hoping he would invite her out again, and he did not disappoint her. They walked uptown along Fifth Avenue, speaking very slowly and intermittently, for almost an hour, then turned east on 55th Street and stopped at a small cafe on the corner of Third Avenue. Inside he led her to a table in the rear, and both looked up briefly at a dark reproduction of absinthe drinkers before taking their uncomfortable-looking ironwork chairs. They ordered drinks and he asked her, abruptly, if she had ever dated an older man. The question seemed to her, if only for a moment, just a bit silly, though she could not have said why. Did he mean to ask, she inquired, whether she had ever had a conversation with an older man? If so, the answer was yes, she had. There were several older men at her office with whom she sometimes spoke, though with none of them had she tried to speak French. And what, he went on, did she think of sexual relations between older men and younger women? Did she regard them as more than a little pathetic, as inevitably sad and hopeless? He confessed that they had always seemed so to him, though in France they were rarely regarded as such, and in New York they were more and more common. He realized, he assured her, that the question would make her very uncomfortable, but he was determined all the same to put it to her, in the interests of candor, so that she might know what he had been thinking for several weeks, and thinking more or less incessantly since the evening they spent together a few nights before. And he was so eager to hear her out on this that he would even consent to dropping their agreement about speaking only French and permit her to speak English if she preferred. This was generous, she observed, though under the circumstances he could hardly expect her to thank him, and in fact, whatever it cost her, she would continue to communicate with him only in French, *merci bien*. If that meant that there was only so much he could hope to know of her feelings and her thoughts, well, so much would have to suffice.

Beyond that, she knew not quite what she wished to say, and nothing in the cafe rose up or intervened to spare her distress. Fumbling, retreating, smiling nervously, she conveyed at last that she had no "position" at all on the question he had raised, probably because it had never occurred to her to consider relations between older men and younger women as a category distinct from other kinds of relationship. And anyhow, where sex was concerned, no views were to be trusted. If you were turned on (she tried variants of *to light, to excite, to combust* on her way to this observation), your ideas about older men were beside the point. She did not see that he had quite grasped all of this, but he seemed pleased, and so she went on to assure him that she was flattered (here she resorted to several English words) to be thought desirable by so seasoned a veteran as her "elderly" interlocutor. All the same, she was far from ready to consider sexual relations with someone she hardly knew, and who in any case interested her without in the least turning her on — *pas encore*.

On their walk further up Third Avenue a bit later he returned to her "amusing" objection to so much as considering sexual relations with someone she hardly knew. How well would she need to know him, he asked, before he merited such consideration? But she was tired, and he soon apologized for what she might take for pressure, when he wanted simply to exercise her French, and to introduce her to the arts of playful conversation. There was no need to respond to this, he assured her, though of course she was free to respond if she wished. He had noted, he said, that her expressive face and her alertness were not at all matched by any corresponding verbal wit or aggression. Oh he knew she was but an intermediate student of French, but he could tell that she was not much accustomed to verbal thrust and parry, and that in the course of their evening together she had surprised herself with the sharpness, the aptness of her responses. There was, in what she had uttered, here and there, *un esprit, une humeur austere,* that she would do well to cultivate. And if he was not to be—at least *pas encore*—her sexual instructor, he was surely willing to be not merely her language teacher but her private tutor in life. He would do his best to bring her out. And wasn't that just as her very own Henry James would have put it? She thought that likely, but she couldn't at all see why he assumed she wanted, or needed, to be brought out. And she was so close to taking most of what he'd said all evening as a series of barely concealed insults that she thought it best to say, at last, though without so much as a breath of reproach, good night.

II.

By the time she took her seat on a budget flight to Orly Airport many months later she had accepted that she did indeed wish to be instructed and brought out. M. LeSaux had done well by her as a language instructor, but he had failed rather miserably to inspire confidence in his likely merits as lover or confidant. Within a week of their third excursion together she had decided not to go out with him again, and he had accepted her decision with admirable coolness, never again pursuing her after class, and pressing her in class no more aggressively than he pressed other students. Again and again in the remaining months of her language course she silently rehearsed their tart exchanges, and she concluded that she had refused him because she was afraid of him and because the intensity of their linguistic play was just "too much" for her. She was—so she felt, even in her middle twenties—a realist, and was not about to demand of herself what she did not have. If she had shown flashes of a certain *esprit*, or finesse, or whatever else it might have been, that was not sufficient reason to revise her sense of her abilities. She would learn to do well enough within her limitations. That was precisely how she put it to herself. She was a person of a particular disposition. She did not think herself impressive, but she was better than others who had taken their lives in hand, and she had always been determined not to mistake a sexual come-on for an offer of affection or concern. To some she may have seemed a babe in the woods, or a tight little puritan, but she was no fool, and she would not be mocked or used.

Her first weeks in Paris were predictably difficult and consoling. She roomed with an old school friend in Montrouge for nearly a month while trying to find an apartment, and she succeeded in lining up one job interview after another without receiving a single offer. At the studio apartment walk-up she soon rented on Rue Versailles near the Bois de Boulogne she lost her key on the first day, before she'd been out to make a copy, and was insulted by the concierge for her carelessness and incompetence. She tossed a one-franc piece in the hat of a neatly-dressed beggar-accordionist in the Metro and had it thrown back at her, apparently because the toss had seemed to convey derision or distaste. (So her friend had explained when asked to speculate on the causes of her singular failure in the Metro.) At the American Hospital, where she'd gone to get help with what looked like an incipient yeast infection, she was referred to a gynecologist at an address that did not exist. The funds she'd had wired to a Credit Lyonnais in her Paris neighborhood were held up, and she was unable to draw on her own account for several weeks. Everything seemed so entirely to conspire against her that she had no choice but to laugh at each new mishap, and she rejoiced each night in her fundamental sanity and her capacity to absorb defeat. The weather was mild, the boulevards brimming and restless. She believed that she had prospects, and she was so utterly ignorant about what lay before her that she imagined good was as likely soon to befall her as ill.

Small signs, as they say, were taken for wonders: one day the concierge smiled warmly at her as she trudged past him on the narrow stairwell, and the ugly dog next door who woke her every morning at six by barking desperately suddenly fell silent. She allowed herself to hope the animal had been run down by a streetcar and that its owner would be too grief-stricken even to consider a replacement. She was not in love, but Paris seemed to her a place that might allow her to feel sated without attachment. She read Brillat-Savarin and decided that the preparation of *haute cuisine* was well within the compass of her disposition and her gifts. With the first withdrawal she made from her transferred bank funds she bought an enormous copper frying pan and cooked an omelette that would have brought tears of joy to the eyes of André Malraux. Quite improbably, she thought herself happy.

After she-didn't-know-how-many interviews she landed a job with an International Institute for Educational Exchange. Though her formal training had prepared her for rather a different position, in business, she eagerly took up her new responsibilities and worked cheerfully in the extra-hours training program to which she was assigned. In a matter of months she was given an office of her own, a private secretary and a staff automobile. Though the automobile—a new pale green Renault with see-through plastic covers on the seats—promptly proved a lemon, repairs were taken care of by the company, and parking was so difficult in her neighborhood that she almost wished the car would remain at the mechanic's indefinitely when she routinely drove it in for an adjustment. She negotiated the Metro system like a native, and in a few months her accent had become good enough almost to allow her to pass for *une Parisienne*. She had a little trouble understanding certain references and phrases in *Le Monde*, but she kept up dutifully and soon participated in lunch conversations and cocktail hours without fear or reticence. At a public meeting in Nanterre she stood up and asked a long question which elicited a heated and elaborate response. Her most optimistic sense of herself was rapidly confirmed. She was a person who tried. She could pass. In the end she might even be said to have come through.

Though she had never thought herself a beauty, her mother had often assured her that she was "attractive." American friends called her "cute," and she supposed a time would come when she would have to settle for "handsome." At a time when many of her contemporaries disdained couture she studied fashion magazines on the sly and always found the money to have her hair done once a week. In Paris she quickly located a reliable beautician on the Boulevard Haussmann a block from Printemps. She shopped for clothing in discount boutiques but usually ended up with stolid, now and then pastel-coloured suits purchased at more expensive shops in the Marais. As in the past, she was complimented on her good taste and too often heard it said that her clothing would never go out of fashion. Quite rightly she took this to mean that her suits were at best respectable and that, if she didn't watch out, she would soon look like a 40-year-old mother of three with all the imagination and high style of a vigilant bank teller. Now and then she experimented with a mauve lipstick and a three-inch-long pair of earrings, but usually she wore pale lipsticks and showed a marked preference for what her mother had primly called the tried and the true. Paris had made her more conscious of fashion than she had been in New York, but she was not about to dress up for the likes of Alain Delon or bid fair to become the latest nocturnal companion of Valery Giscard D' Estaing. She would work to enhance her regular features and clear complexion, her serene hazel eyes and her slender, unimpeachable figure. If more were demanded she would surely resist.

After eight months with the International Institute she was sent for a weekend conference to Nice, where she met a man she wanted to marry. This desire, so unexpected, so definite, seemed to her absurdly premature. Walter was a dark, serious man with a neatly trimmed beard and a three-piece, rust-coloured corduroy suit he must have bought in the United States or, just possibly, in Vienna. He wore a sports watch with a multitude of irrelevant features and had so much to say on so many different subjects that one soon felt he didn't know how to keep quiet. An American by birth, he was the senior member of the French "team" assembled for the Nice conference, and had been a program administrator for several years. She asked his advice on one tactical question after another, and laughed compulsively at his practiced jokes and clever anecdotes. On their first evening he took her arm as they entered the formal dining room at the Hotel de Ville, and he kissed her on both cheeks when they said good night in the lobby several hours later. Seated next to him at the long conference table the following morning, she admired his meticulously prepared notes and his thoughtfully furrowed brows. He spoke with impressive authority and reserve about the extension of their program to sectors of the French population rarely represented in educational exchange. He spoke of monetary costs and social costs, of opportunity and responsibility, and he seemed to her to understand perfectly the difference between making a serious proposal and making a speech. The distinction had never seemed to her so clear, or so important, before, and she was grateful to him for rapidly confirming her impression that she had never before gotten close to so substantial a man. If, as she had also felt, her attraction to Walter was premature and probably unhealthy, he was, clearly, a man who might truly bring her out. It did not occur to her that she might do anything for him.

On the flight back to Paris on Sunday evening they managed to sit together, and he complained greedily to her that he was stuck in a job he had known for some time to be unworthy of him. This struck her as surprising—the uttered confidence was so sudden, so intimate—and also sad, but the situation seemed to her not nearly as hopeless as he had suggested. Convinced after a weekend with him that he might accomplish anything he set his mind to, she would have been astonished to hear that, like her, he was subject to "limitations," and furious at the suggestion that he exaggerated his merits. She defended him against himself at every turn, though he accused himself of nothing, and spoke of his "just getting out" as if he might move with no difficulty to another equally well-paid position. He clearly approved of her solicitousness and spent two hours searching her face for any sign of irony or dispassion. This she noted as he continued to pour out his complaints and even on one occasion to anxiously squeeze her hand. Too embroiled in their soulful exchange to look up, they allowed the beverage and sandwich carts to pass them in the aisle and ignored the seatbelt warnings as the plane was about to set down. She could not remember receiving so urgent and plaintive a confidence before—certainly not from a man—and he surely wondered—so his slightly stunned expression now and then betrayed—at the welling up of a woe he had assiduously kept to himself. Anyone studying the two of them there on the routine tourist-class flight would have seen at once that they were embarked on an intimacy that held them utterly.

The courtship was exemplary. They took lunch together every day and met every evening—early or late—after work. She refused to give up her apartment and move into his place before they were married, but within a few days of their Nice weekend they were sleeping together. She thought him an excellent lover, and he expressed such gratitude and affection that she thought herself quite expert as well. He consulted her on professional matters and on the serge suit he had long wanted to buy. When she asked him to come to the phone and say hello to her mother he introduced himself at such length and spoke of his passionate love of her daughter with such obvious joy and sincerity that she found herself speechless when at last he returned the phone to her. At the apartment of his closest friend on rue de Lafayette he soon placed her on his lap and offered to share with her the cognac he sipped after dinner. He referred to her as "my dear," and she thought herself delectable. Again and again she encouraged him to take a new position if he was unhappy in his work, but she believed that he could make his present job worthy of him. She arranged for him to have a private lunch with Ivan Illych when the flamboyant guru consulted with the Institute in Paris for a few days, and things went so well that Walter took her shopping for shoes at Arche later the same afternoon. They talked about moving to a new apartment the following year, and they speculated about opening an agency of their own to accomplish what was done with considerable inefficiency and waste at the Institute that paid their salaries. He praised her daring and her steadiness. She told him he was the sexiest man she had ever met and that it was a consummate pleasure to watch him trim his beard and step out of his pants. She was—both were—in all things deferential and full of apparent good cheer. His complaining ceased, and she thought him to be in every way adequate and wise.

Now and then they spoke of Paris, of the vicissitudes that had led them to abandon everything for a city they had only read about and a language that had earlier seemed an obstacle to every prospect. Neither had traveled when they were children, neither had grown up worldly or adaptable. In high school both had chosen Spanish as the more useful language, but both had been stirred by the wayward and eccentric figures they met in French films. He had imagined himself in a car with Godard's "married woman" driving past the statues in the Louvre gardens. Her fantasies ran more towards the girlfriends of Truffaut's Antoine Doinel. She liked the sound of Antoine's name and pronounced it with him aloud when he spoke it on screen. Both admitted to having felt bored with Alain Resnais' *Hiroshima, Mon Amour* and to having understood almost nothing of Godard's *2 or 3 Things I Know About Her*. But they remembered how sophisticated they felt about sex and politics when they saw *La Guerre Est Finis*. Yes, of course he had wanted to be like Yves Montand, and yes, she had thought revolutionary politics both preposterous and wonderful. To be French, they had felt, was to understand life in a way that was fundamentally unavailable to Americans. Both knew well enough that not every Frenchman was an Yves Montand, and she was surely bright enough even as a college girl to see that the young revolutionaries in Godard's *La Chinoise* were silly, if also somehow appealing. She had never really wanted to be a young Frenchwoman, not until she found her adult life in New York disappointing, but it now seemed to her that the seeds of her obsession were planted in the evenings she spent watching movies. Though Walter's attachment was of longer duration and probably went deeper, he had been through what seemed to him a comparable process. They spoke as if Paris now meant to them a great deal more than it could have meant earlier, but they were reluctant to claim anything like a romantic infatuation with the place. By the time they were tired of talking, yet again, of Paris, they reflected, yet again, that Paris had brought them together and that naturally they would speak of it always. And what precisely was the understanding of life that came so readily to the French, and probably not at all to Americans? It was enough that both felt they knew, though neither could say.

III.

In 1980, after several years of marriage and the birth of two children, she woke up one morning and declared, silently, that Walter had not brought her out, though he had been to her everything she asked of him, and at no time had he accused her of having failed to uphold her end of the marital bargain. They were bent on raising their children as privileged young Parisians, and together strove to enroll them in the best French nursery schools and to surround them with every advantage. They entertained rather lavishly in their comfortable apartment facing Parc Monceau, and they counted among their friends a government minister, a cultural *attache*, several accomplished writers and a brilliant though still relatively unknown documentary filmmaker. Walter's name had figured in several newspaper stories on educational exchange, and she had been asked to co-edit a newsletter put out by the Institute. It was unthinkable that she should hold Walter or anyone else accountable for what she took to be deficiencies in a life others would envy. She had no right to feel dissatisfied. So she believed. To invoke a "failure" to be brought out was to indulge the worst kind of anachronistic nonsense.

For what, in truth, was entailed in the desire to be brought out? Did it not entail, in the first place, a desire to have someone else do for you what you were presumably unable to do for yourself? And suppose that Walter had somehow managed to change her. Might she then have worried about his declining self esteem? By any standard she could name Walter was quite alright, but hardly grand, and the truth was, he was not quite the man he had earlier taken himself to be.

Their choice of Paris and of everything French was clearly an element in her disappointment. Oddly, she did not think that an American woman of her generation would indulge quite the same complaints. She imagined that, as an American, she would by this point in her life have securely dismissed as nonsense the very idea that one might be changed as a result of another's investment. And she would have taken as comforting signs of modesty and proportion the contentment she routinely felt in the life she had made. Her restlessness now made her feel that she had been infected with a peculiarly French *folie*, a species of derangement she associated with culturally ingrained delusions of grandeur.

Of course it was also possible that her unease was related to a suspicion — she had tried to ignore it for months — that Walter was increasingly desperate. He had remained with the Institute, had made the most of opportunities available to him in what was, finally, a minor operation. Others might have taken pride in accomplishing so much with so little. He blamed himself for staying, occasionally spoke of his weakness and timidity. He took pleasure — so he said — in working together with her, in their long lunches and special shared initiatives. He liked being commissioned by her to write something for the newsletter, liked "approving" her travel vouchers. If he was desperate, he did his best not to seem so. He played almost obsessively with the children for an hour or so after dinner on evenings when they were able to take their meals *en famille*, and he obviously enjoyed their springtime frolics in the gardens at Versailles and the Sunday summer afternoon concerts at Sceaux. He marveled openly about all that Paris allowed them to offer the children, and never failed to compare the relative safety of the Paris Metro to the New York City subway system they had both feared and abhorred.

To see the desperation one had to catch him at odd moments, when he had forgotten to marvel, or compare, or praise. One evening after the children had gone to bed, she observed him seated at his elegant writing table just off their bedroom in the small study they shared. He had been seated there for about a half hour, with neither books nor papers open before him. He had been fingering through documents in his briefcase, taking nothing out, peering in as though looking for something in particular, but clearly distracted and benumbed. She was about to ask him what he was looking for, whether she could help, but stopped herself, aware suddenly that he knew no better than she what he hoped to find. Against the desperation she observed she was helpless to recommend anything. But it did come upon her with a certain force that, if anything was to be done about her own disappointment, it would be initiated and sustained not by Walter but by herself. The thought led to no new resolve, and she soon set aside her unease the better to contend with his.

IV.

At her daughter's sixteenth birthday party she was struck again by how many friends they had accumulated. She had been in Paris for so long that it did not occur to her to wonder why it was necessary to invite them all. In New York perhaps one or two would have been invited, along with Nicole's friends and the inevitable relatives. As it was, only the fact that Nicole had a summer birthday allowed them to throw so grand a fete. The cramped apartment into which she'd lately moved with the girls would never have accommodated so many people, but the ample garden just below the Avenue de Tilleuls was perfect for their purposes. The girls were delighted with their place in Chatou, and didn't at all mind traveling twenty minutes to their school in Paris on the RER train. Friends who'd already visited her in Chatou thought she was fortunate to be outside Paris, and said she'd get used to the small rooms in no time. They said she was fortunate to be able to open her windows onto the Seine and to look across to the stately trees mounted just on the other side of the river on the Ile des Impresionistes. Walter's place was nearby, in the next town downriver, and the girls could see him whenever they wished. He would ride over on his bike for the party. So he'd told her in the morning when she phoned to remind him about the *terrine au saumon* he'd promised to bring.

She was still uncomfortable about the arrangement with Walter. She never knew whether to refer to him as her husband or as her ex-husband. Legally they remained married, and he had assured her that if it were up to him there would be no need ever to alter that arrangement. He loved her, would always love her, and the children would of course always be the children of their marriage. If they needed to live apart and to see less of each other than they had become accustomed to, that was no reason to behave as if a catastrophe had occurred. When they made love, once or twice a week at his place, he was as considerate as he had ever been, and she did not often permit herself to think about where he had picked up the little variations and grace notes he had begun to introduce into a pattern that had seemed perfectly satisfactory before. Once or twice she almost regretted having no new posture or device of her own to offer, and hoped that she might be clever enough to think them up when she could bring herself to try. Occasionally she wept during their lovemaking, and Walter was then unfailingly generous, talking her through her distress, coaxing her back to the enjoyment of his body. Always she was grateful to him then, and she took some pride in their never having given up and parted before they had completed what they had begun. He was perhaps not really her husband any more, but she would hold on to what there was.

As she greeted arriving guests in the first hour of their party she was irritated that Walter had not yet arrived. Their friends would assume that he was not coming, and when he did finally walk in he would look as if he had just stopped by to do her and his daughters a favor. Oh he'd be gracious and friendly. He'd embrace her and kiss them all as if he were anything but an occasional visitor. But he'd let them know, all the same, that he had set himself apart and was doing exceedingly well, thank you very much, in his well-appointed bachelor's apartment in Croissy. No doubt he'd even go so far as to invite some of the guests to drop in on him at his place some other time. He would make himself instantly at home in her apartment, of course, would take what he liked from the refrigerator and help himself to the brandy on the high shelf in the kitchen cabinet as if it were his kitchen. He would refer to her casually as *ma femme* and express pride in her *boulettes* and her *coquille St. Jacques*. For all to see it would be as if he had never left.

When Walter did arrive the party was well along, quite as she'd imagined, but she'd already downed two glasses of Chablis and was briefly amused as he muttered his apologies and made the rounds. She stood beside the buffet table and watched him, noting that he looked better, more youthful, in his dark beard and ample moustache, than he'd looked a year earlier when his clean-shaven face had seemed gaunt and sallow. She could tell that for the first time in his life he had begun to think himself terribly attractive to women, and she could not but consider in contrast how much she had lately aged and coarsened. Her hips had broadened, shallow age lines had begun to appear in her upper lip. Every three weeks she had her hair colored at a shop in Chatou. A few nights before the party, as they lay together exhausted in his bed, she'd laughed when she told him he might at least have had the decency to lose his hair before leaving his family. She was surprised that he didn't find that at all funny, though she guessed he would have laughed had she said the same thing in front of their friends at the buffet table.

In a while a large group had formed around Nicole, who answered questions about her future and sometimes turned to her father for confirmation or advice. Would she leave Paris in a year or two to study at an American university? Her father had thought she might, she said, though she was as yet uncertain. And had she any opinion on what she was apt to find at an American university that she would not find in Paris? The conversation moved easily around the room, one voice following another, Nicole entertained, Walter glibly solicitous. No one seemed to notice that the mistress of the house was decidedly out of the conversation, that she sat some distance away from the charmed circle, a fixed smile frozen on her face, her younger daughter Sidie seated on the grass at her feet. Now and then Sidie smiled up at her, and she reached down to stroke her auburn hair or caressed her back with her bare foot. It occurred to her that no one had said anything interesting about French life, that for all these ardent French types knew, Nicole might well find in the United States only what she'd find in Paris. For what would she be looking, after all? Would she, like her mother, be looking for a man to make a life for her? If so, she would be as disappointed in the one place as in the other. Or would she perhaps fancy herself a modern young woman and refuse to think of men as anything but incidental to the experience she sought? Paris and New York could be equally treacherous and inhospitable places, and she hoped that Nicole would permit her mother to protect her, at least from undue suffering and unreasonable hope.

At other moments, when Walter held forth volubly on cultural differ-ence, she reflected bitterly on the emptiness of the entire business and considered that it didn't really matter what Nicole eventually did with her life or where she went to study. She herself had devoted most of her adult life to a Parisian experience, and where had it gotten her? There wasn't re-ally much that could be done with her hair or with the long-suffering look she saw in her own face and imagined others saw there as well. She had mastered the language of the French and taken to heart all their codes and verities. Her husband, likewise, had abandoned his allegiance to things American and tried to become in every sense a Frenchman, but was he a better man for it? Did he think more clearly, love more deeply, care more passionately for anything but himself? She didn't think there had been much of a gain. And besides, after all the trouble he'd taken, Walter had to notice that their friends continued to think of them as Americans at heart: their daughters would naturally be drawn to the states. She had half a mind to ask them if perhaps they did not trust Nicole's ac-cent, or thought her parents carried themselves like tourists. Walter would not have cared for those questions, would have thought them in poor taste.

In fact, she had found herself more and more often provoking Walter with what he took to be absurdities. He thought it idiotic to dwell on un-savory details of French life or, indeed, on the collective psychology of the French. She, on the other hand, showed a growing talent for skepti-cism and denial that could issue in cynicism and cruelty. It did her good to see Walter squirm when she remarked on the stench of French bodies in the local market or in the lobby of the Paris opera at intermission. She spoke often of things she knew little about, and once went so far as to ask Walter how bureaucrats like themselves could have any feeling for what was original and dangerous in *la Belle France*. Oh she knew she was trad-ing in commonplaces and clichés. She knew that she sometimes struck blindly and instinctively and without much caring what she hit. How did she know what most bureaucrats admired? Or Frenchmen? If she was miserable, did that mean that Walter had no right to make his own life more bearable? She hated all of these questions, and could not quite believe that no one would help her with them.

When the party ended she sat alone on a stool at the kitchen counter staring up at her fine copper pots hanging on the wall. Nicole had helped with the cleanup and had been the last to leave—on a last-minute date. Sidie was already asleep in her room, where Walter had deposited her before he drove off to who knows what waiting for him elsewhere. She had looked at him with unconcealed revulsion as the party drew to a close, and her friend Agnes had taken her aside to whisper that other guests had noticed. She had muttered to Agnes something about the *haute* bullshit of Parisian wit, dryness and proportion, and was pleased to note that Walter overheard her when she described his oh-so-French attraction to freedom as a conviction that he was entitled to separate from his family and to take a consort younger than his wife without suffering any pain. She was struck by the bitterness of her words and sick of her increasing need to whine and to confide in people who had no wish to be confided in. The party, which had its moments of hilarity, now seemed to her rather sordid and grim, and she blamed herself for having put Nicole through a difficult day. At several moments in the course of the party Nicole had assured her mother that it was alright to "act up"—Walter said she meant "act out"— but Nicole was always sweet and supportive, and obviously didn't yet grasp the blackness of her mother's anger.

By the time Nicole had come home and gone to bed, her mother had downed two sobering cups of black coffee and wondered whether she'd ever again get to sleep. The tiny apartment was as presentable as it was going to be, and she looked dumbly at the occasional boat, lights blinking, passing below on the Seine. She remembered that she had once thought lights on the Seine an emblem of the France she loved, quite as the open-to-the-public fifth floor cafeteria and late hours of the Musee Pompidou seemed to her a token of French generosity and forward thinking. Had these wonderful things ever seemed wonderful in the same way to Walter? Walter had been sustained by none of these things, she felt, and she had come gradually to doubt them all in the degree that they seemed, one after another, to be of no enduring consequence to him. She did not like to admit to him that she was in the process of losing what only he could give back to her, though at moments her disaffection and hurt could seem almost eloquent.

Of course she never really understood why she had not severed her ties earlier, beaten Walter to the punch, maybe—before it was suddenly too late—demanded that he damn it once and for all acknowledge the pathetic failure of their twenty-year-long French experiment. Certainly it would have seemed a demand fraught with recrimination, even then, when he still thought her his mainstay. And no doubt he would have brought up to her the skill with which she shifted onto him the burden of acknowledging failure when it was her own timidity she might rather have confronted. Had she ever really wanted to be brought out? She might have suspected even earlier that really she had not the ambition, let alone the stomach. From the perspective of her dim little kitchen in Chatou she thought it just as well that they'd never had the climactic shoot-out, that they'd waited in semiconsciousness for the succession of ever more dully inexorable footfalls to overtake them.

When she had folded out the living room couch at last, and smiled to think that this was apt to be a ritual she confronted every night for a long time to come, she opened an old copy of Janet Flanner's *Paris Was Yesterday* and hoped it would calm her. She lay down on the ample mattress fully clothed, propped a pillow behind her head, and looked around at the motley assortment of things she had used to decorate the walls. There were amateur sketches of Nicole and Sidie executed in pencil by a young friend who'd done them in an hour or so one night at dinner in Chatou. There were the impossible Audubon bird posters she and the girls had picked up at an Audubon exhibit at the Grand Palais in the spring. There was an improbable reproduction of a tawny Japanese wood-block print, depicting a young child clinging to the back of its mother, who bent over to comb her lustrous black hair. She had never looked closely at this im-

age, which Sidie had brought home after a class visit to a collection of
Asian art. It might have held her longer had she not been drawn to the
large antique map of Provence Walter had insisted she take from their
Paris apartment. It was handsomely framed, and as she looked at it she
noted that it named places they had once planned to explore. They had
done a week in and around Avignon years earlier, when she announced
to Walter that the remote history of France was not even remotely interesting to her. She remembered too that she and Nicole had both suffered
from motion sickness on their daily excursions in a rented Peugeot whose
cooling system unfailingly drove currents of hot air into the car. The elegant map seemed to her to betray nothing but an inhuman, abstract elegance, and she suddenly hated it and vowed as she closed her eyes to take
the thing down and let Walter have it. The book slipped, unread, from her
fingers onto the floor.

Secrets and Sons

You see, he said. I'm turning my face to the wall. This was more than a figure of speech. He sank into the hospital bed, turned away and closed his eyes, shutting me out. He was finished with me, played out. I turn away from you, he was saying in the only way he could. I renounce you and all your courtesies and condolences. I give you up and ask that you do no less for me. Witness me not. Learn to do without the slow spectacle of my diminishment and dying. Learn that I am not for you and you will understand that you are not for me.

It had not always been so. A month earlier he had seemed to welcome my visits, my calls, the postcards I sent him when work required that I be away for a week or longer. At the nursing home the dozens of postcards were neatly wrapped in rubber bands at his bedside, the prettiest ones, as he called them, tacked to the walls. His lean, hairless head had a gaunt authority, even with his body covered in a sheet all the way up to his chin. Often he memorized the cards I'd sent and asked me pertinent questions to show he was tuned in. Who was with you on the trip to Rome? You didn't say. Did you ever finish the story you started on the plane, about the guy who has a fatal encounter in the parking lot? See, he would say, how carefully I read you? I hang in there, don't I, even here, at the final outpost, the faithful catheter ever in place, my waking hours down to four or five at most. But you can still make me laugh. Tell me a good one and I'll laugh at all the right places. You'll see.

He had been slipping for at least a year, even before he went into the nursing home. How ever did we meet? he asked me one night, months earlier.

You don't remember? I replied. But it's obvious, isn't it? That we met long ago when I reviewed your poems and asked you to write something for the magazine?

And did I? he asked, still searching, not visibly anxious, willing to be forgetful, very much at his ease in his wheelchair, his checkered flannel shirt collar open at the hollow throat, no big deal if you can't remember things, right?

Of course you wrote, I assured him, a long article, just as I expected.

And was it good? he asked.

It was very good, I told him.

That makes sense, he said, that it was good.

But you don't remember it at all?

Must not have been very important, he said. Magazine pieces come and go, don't they? Not like my po-ems, he said, separating the parts of the word, stretching out each syllable as he often did to lightly mock the very idea that he should have devoted so much of his life to po-ems. Slight, useless things, he often said, especially when he'd just completed a new one and was handing it to me. It ain't much, he'd say. Just give it a look when there's nothing else to do.

Once, at the tail end of a bad couple of days in the nursing home, when he seemed distracted and depressed, his fingers clutching at his bed-clothes, his bowels "acting up again," I asked if he wanted me to read to him.

Nope, he said.

I can read you a very short story I just read for the first time myself.

Fuck the story, he said.

Should I put on some music?

Read me a po-em, he said.

I didn't bring any with me, I said.

Get me started, then, he commanded. Start me up with something I know.

Who by? I asked.

Someone, he answered. Anyone.

Lowell? I asked. Robert Lowell?

Like what? he asked.

"For the Union Dead"? "The Quaker Graveyard"?

How does that one go?

A brackish reach of shoal off Madaket, I began, very deliberately, but I could go no further, and didn't need to, his thin, delicate lips already stepping on my line, repeating the opening words and going on to deliver without a hitch the entire thing, page after page, the music filling the little room, the frail voice again, briefly, a fine instrument tuned to produce every slightest roll and inflection, until, finished at last, he lay back against the pillow, his eyes closed, the mouth fixed in an improbable smile of triumph and relief. It's there, isn't it? he asked. It's all there, whatever else is lost to me.

But in a while he no longer recited anything, not even the Passover songs I asked him to sing with me on the first seder night when we sat again at his bedside and my wife Phyllis presented him with a plate of potato pancakes and a very small bottle of Manischewitz wine. No songs, he said. No poems. He seemed to be disappearing before our eyes. My wife would hold his hand while he stared mostly away, not in pain, clearly, or in distress, but vacant, adrift.

We'll be away in Venice, I said, for only a week this time, like I told you on the phone.

In Venice? he vaguely intoned, as if awakening from sleep.

Exactly, I said, just long enough to see the Biennale and take our niece to dinner a couple of times.

Lots of water, he said, and bridges. I remember the bridges, and pigeon shit. You know it's bound to smell. It's your first time, yes?

No, not the first, I said.

I thought it was, he whispered, but his voice trailed off, and there was no use reminding him that we'd been there for a conference seven months earlier and that he had on his night table ten or twelve postcards I'd mailed him, one for each day of that previous trip to a place my wife liked better than any other.

To my surprise Lennie then walked in. Dark glasses, a single rhinestone earring, lots of attitude. We hadn't seen him in months, and it was clear he stayed away whenever we were scheduled to visit Irving. Didn't want to see us, we figured, or to sit through the long silences when we'd all pretend we just happened momentarily to run out of things to say.

The old man says you're leaving town, he said. Another pleasure trip, I guess.

That's it, I said. Some people live for pleasure, others because they can't think of anything else to do.

Lennie was a loyal kid but he gave me a pain. Of course he wasn't a kid any more, nearly forty by now, handsome in a slack sort of way, with a big open mouth and thick purplish lips. His skin was very dark, his arms hung at his sides like ropes, his legs slightly bowed, so that you wouldn't think of him as a fine specimen, not at all, though firm, attractive in his way.

How'd you get here so early? Irving asked him.

Just took off early from work, Lennie said, 'cause I felt like it. I figured if these two can take off whenever they want and fly off somewhere, why the hell can't I take off for a change? Anyone got trouble with that?

It's a treat to see you, Phyllis said.

No it ain't, he said. But it's nice of you to say it.

She's always nice, and she always means what she says, Irving interjected. He was alert enough to have caught some tension in the air and he wanted to nip it before it got out of hand. They're going to Venice, Lennie.

I know that, he said, 'cause you told me, old man. Just 'cause you forget don't mean a black guy can't remember things.

Has nothing to do with black, Irving said, or white. I used to remember everything, then I didn't.

Lennie stood at the bedside, his thumbs now hooked into the pockets

Excitable Women, Damaged Men

of his jeans, rocking a little bit as if working himself up to something. Came over to tell you I got the whole thing under control, so you can go away and not have a worry.

We count on you, Phyllis said. Always do.

He's my son, Irving said. Like a son but better.

And I ain't gonna let him forget it, Lennie said, 'cause he ain't got nothin' else.

Well, not exactly nothing, I said. If I'd been smoking I'd have blown a mouthful in his face just then, but instead I just said, Irv's a lucky man.

Lennie laughed at that, showed me a mouthful of teeth and slapped the bedpost for emphasis. You always say the thing you don't mean to say, he said, playful but malicious, a trace of scorn in his voice, a little high-pitched for a big broad man but with unmistakable force.

I was relieved when he left ten minutes later. He's great, Phyllis said. He looks great and he is great.

Gives me a pain, I said.

Makes you tense, Irving suggested. I can feel it in the air whenever you're together in a room.

Lennie had left behind, as he always did, a pungent smell of cologne. Once I'd suggested, mildly, that maybe he was a bit too lavish in applying the stuff. I like it, he said. Guys like it, you know what I mean, guys.

Whatever works, I replied. Just trying to be helpful.

You're a regular good Samaritan, he said, always lookin' out for someone else's interest.

I'd never seen Lennie with another black man. His companions were invariably white, well-proportioned, usually better looking than Lennie and apparently better educated too. One favorite companion was an environmental lawyer, another a history teacher. Lennie had barely managed to get through high school and was a road worker for the New Paltz department of public works. At one point he wore a variety of gay pride emblems on his tee shirts and around his squat neck, but Irving didn't at all care for that sort of thing and asked him to cut it out. No problem, he said, if it bothers you. I liked that best about Lennie, that he could yield to Irving that way, though he didn't have to. When he wanted to have a tattoo burned into his bicep he all but asked Irving's permission, and Irving had said, so long as it's discreet, it's your decision. Your decision anyway.

They were, to put it mildly, an odd couple. Lennie couldn't read his way through any of Irving's poems, not even the one dedicated to him. Gives me a fuckin' headache, Lennie said. I read my name there on the page under the title and that's enough.

Of course they were not in any sexual sense a couple. They had been, both of them, abused children, Irving by an older brother, Lennie by an uncle over the course of six or eight adolescent years. The story had run in a local paper and led to Irving's taking an interest in the boy, who delivered his groceries. When I first met the kid he was eighteen and living under the care of some child welfare agency, still delivering groceries and hanging out on Irving's front porch in the summer months. He was, Irving told me, sexually unresolved at the time and Irving was bound and determined to get him through his ambivalence.

I remember, Irving suddenly said, shifting in his bed and turning on the light, when you liked each other.

He never liked me, I said. Mistrusted me from the first. Sorry, but facts are facts.

He looked up to you, Irving corrected. He envied you. Your confidence and all. Your wife. Even that. He had nothing and you had everything. That's not mistrust.

Nothing to be done about it now, I said. Mistrust, envy, whatever, he's got his settled view and he enjoys going with it. I trigger a whole reaction formation in him. I can see it building the second he lays eyes on me.

Big words, Irving said. Reaction formation. Good thing Lennie's not around.

For a brief time I'd thought maybe Irving had his eye on Lennie not merely as a reclamation project. But then he hurried along Lennie's relations with a big heavy-boned blonde girl who was poor and eager and sweet. Good for him, Irving said, to settle down with someone who'll look up to him and set him straight. She was, I thought, a girl who would have been fast had she found young men to take an interest in her.

As it was, Lennie got her to marry him after they'd dated for maybe three months. Phyllis and I reluctantly attended the wedding, where there were in total about a dozen guests and Irving was the best man. Lennie wore one of Irving's sports jackets, a navy blue blazer with brass buttons. His mother, a round woman with skin even blacker than Lennie's, stood well to the side of the action and seemed not to want to be introduced to anyone. The bride wore a white Mexican-style dress that draped her large body like a tent. When she smiled she showed a mouth full of irregularly spaced teeth, and she carried a bouquet of flowers that looked like they'd been freshly picked from the edge of the culvert that ran along Route 28 near the abandoned underwear factory, the blossoms torn and graying.

Within a year this large fertile cow had produced a son, a year later another. Lennie made convincing fatherly noises over and around them and Irving seemed delighted to have inspired the creation of this burgeoning ménage. He bought them a trailer and two acres of land on which to settle it. Lennie did his best to seem grateful. On Thanksgiving he dutifully carved the family turkey and gave thanks to their fastidious benefactor for the abundant bounty they enjoyed. On his second wedding anniversary he asked Irving to babysit and took his wife dancing at a nearby club renowned for watering its drinks and its burnt-to-a-crisp southern fried chicken.

A year later the wife was filing for divorce, citing irreconcilable differences. Lennie was picking up boys and had recently spent two or three nights each week away from home. He hated the trailer and hoped the wife and kids would be happy there on god's two little rocky acres. He'd be happy to leave behind all the Kmart furniture and even the framed prints Irving had given them for the wall above the couch. Just so's I don't have to go back, Lennie said, licking his one gold tooth and playing with the silver chain around his neck. Deliver me, he said, from Kmart and from painted toenails and hair curlers.

Irving never said much about the boys Lennie brought by. He's a nice one, Irving would say. Better looking than the blonde boy. And smart. Taking a graduate degree. But Phyllis speculated that Irving spared us the full extent of Lennie's conquests and campaigns. More than once he'd made disapproving noises about gay men and their ways, though never about Lennie. Little cock teasers, he called them. Or nasty boys. You know what I mean, he'd say.

But I didn't know what he meant, and I wondered why he himself never seemed to have a partner. Had he ever been to bed with anyone? Of course he had, Phyllis said. How can you say that? Do you think he's been celibate all his life just because he doesn't report to you what he's doing? Of course he said, now and then, that he'd been in love once or twice. But it came to nothing, he assured me. Something not quite right in his relations. Whereas guys like you, he said, always know they're normal. Normal? I would ask him. You know, he'd reply, normal as in married with children, and all praise to that, the natural design and all, and don't let anybody tell you different. Once, he said, there had been that dancer, a woman, who would have needed only to snap her fingers for him to come running. She had made a dance from one of his poems, and he insisted that the signed portrait of the grand lady he kept over his office desk—for Irving, all the very best—was a token not of a great failure but of a great creative moment. Though had she, even once, signaled to him that she was ready to receive him in that other way they might have had, the two of them, ecstasies.

In the seventies Irving rented rooms on the upper floor of his New Paltz house to a male pianist who taught at the college a few days each week but had a life in New York. We hoped they were lovers but had nothing from Irving to confirm that. Often they dined together, and occasionally the two of them took us to dinner at a Mexican restaurant. No gestures of intimacy, no hand holdings or casual caresses, nothing to fuel more than idle speculation. Once we stopped by unannounced at Irving's place to drop off a print he'd asked to see. Todd came to the door in his jockey shorts, apparently at his ease, a wine glass in his hand, though he apologized when he saw that Phyllis was with me and quickly wrapped a towel around himself. Irving welcomed us to the "harem," seemed only a little uncomfortable, but he was clearly relieved when we said no thanks, we had no time even for a quick drink.

The New York Times obituary for Todd in 1986 did not give a cause of death. He was 58. We'd noted about a year earlier that he suddenly looked old, ravaged. There were sores on his face. Where's Todd? I asked one day. Gone, Irving said. Gone where? Just gone, he said, so I'm renting to someone else. Is he in touch? I asked. Not lately, he said, and I could see he wanted no further questions on this subject. Was he worried about his own health? If he was he never told us. Phyllis said I owed it to Irving and to myself to ask after Todd again, but that was not my way, certainly not with Irving, who harbored secrets, hugged them to him, a man somehow confiding and inaccessible.

For a time I thought we knew him better than anyone else. It's good to be so well known, he would say. Good when you have no family of your own to have a surrogate son. You're my family, you two, he would say. We're brothers, you and I, and Phyllis is our secret sharer who knows both of us better by far than we know ourselves.

But I never trusted this assessment, never felt I knew all there was to know or that I could handle anything Irving held back. I was afraid to learn things he might tell me about Lennie, or about the life he led when he was young and hung out in Key West with Elizabeth Bishop and other gay poets. Was he, had he ever been a promiscuous man? A cock teaser? In youthful photos he is invariably thin and golden, by no means effeminate-looking but fine featured, even in his dark tee shirt a bit of a dandy. Briefly I imagined him cruising the dark streets for boys, wondered if there were regulars he saw in Key West each winter, or in Haiti and the other places where in later years he rented property for the winter months. As his chosen official biographer I supposed I might one day read his intimate letters and find allusions to lovers, but the thought invariably filled me with an unaccountable dread.

On a warm spring night, when Irving was seventy or so, Phyllis and I circled around the streets of New Paltz searching for a place to park. Soon I gave up, dropped Phyllis in front of a small Italian restaurant and made my way to a municipal parking lot about five blocks away. I walked through the dark back streets, past rundown two- and three-family row houses and ugly littered yards, until I saw, moving ahead of me, what looked like Irving. He moved with a stealthy, halting pace, his large head intermittently visible as he passed under an occasional streetlamp. Of course I'd thought at first to call his name, to stop him, but something told me this was not a good idea. At one point he came to a halt in front of a lone clapboard house, and I moved behind a tree at the edge of the sidewalk to be sure he couldn't turn and see me watching him. He took something from his jacket pocket and seemed to stare at it closely for a time, then went further up the street and turned the corner. When I all but caught up to him halfway up the next street he had stopped again, this time in front of a well-lit bar or small nightclub. A sort of a ramp led up to the door of the establishment, and I saw leaning against the wooden railings on either side of the ramp two young men, their collars open, heads thrown back, hands apparently gripping the railings, garlands of smoke curling from their mouths, visible in the sharp white lights mounted all along the façade of the building. I saw Irving go up the ramp a few steps and exchange words with one of the young men, who took off his glasses and examined Irving as if he'd been assigned to ascertain his identity. Irving withdrew something from his pocket, as he had before, but this time handed it to the young man and took his place against the railing.

It was at that point, leaning back, and with both arms stretched behind to support him, that Irving suddenly turned his head and met my eye. I had not noticed that I was myself standing below a streetlamp not twenty feet away, and when I said Irving, he said at once, what the hell are you doing there? Going to meet Phyllis for dinner at Ciao Bella, I said. But what, he persisted, are you doing on this block staring that way at me?

I'm not staring, I said. Just trying to be sure it's you.

Easy enough, he said, to find that out. He didn't at all shift his position in the course of this exchange, holding his ground, the slightest trace of irritation evident in his tone, his eyes fixed on me, probing, I thought, for some sign of weakness or inclination to flight. So it's me, he said.

So I see.

And is that enough?

It's enough, I said. Unless you want to join us for *vongole*.

I had my dinner, he said, and I can tell you, you won't like the fare they serve in this place.

What's it called? I asked.

Billy's, he said. A bit unsavory, they tell me. Ever hear of it?

Don't think so.

Not for you, he said. Not for Phyllis. Best to put it out of mind. Pretend you didn't run into me.

About an hour later he showed up at our table at Ciao Bella. He looked a little sheepish but pulled up a chair and ordered a margarita. For a while we made small talk about the pasta and the radicchio and the dark extra-virgin olive oil on the table. Had I told her, Irving asked Phyllis, that we met up an hour earlier. What do you think? she replied. You know he tells me everything.

You're like a couple of innocent kids, Irving said. You think there's nothing worth concealing.

Just haven't found it yet, she said.

And what did you make of it? he asked me.

Of what?

Of the place you found me at.

Nothing to make of it, I said. If you want to tell me more I can make something of it.

Not curious? he asked.

Not very, I answered. Should I be?

Nope, he said. Nothing you need to know about.

Of course we inquired about Billy's the next day and learned that it was a gay bar with a by-invitation-only policy, an insider's place to which, no doubt, Irving had been summoned, or invited, by someone he chose not to mention that night. Possibly he'd been invited by Lennie, at the time not much more than twenty and definitely not "out," though no doubt he got around even then. The club was hardly an exclusive night spot catering to an upscale clientele. Irving's early departure from the place, I guessed, probably had to do with the seedy surroundings and unappetizing guests.

On the other hand, Phyllis said, he may have gotten exactly what he went for and left the minute he was through.

You must be joking, I said.

Sorry to offend you with the obvious, she said.

Often I told myself that had Irving wanted me to know more about him, I'd have overcome my reluctance and pressed him. But Irving's misgivings about things sexual were at least as pronounced as my own reluctance to get inside the steamier aspects of his life. Maybe he considered me conventional, puritanical, and played to that, thinking me a friend only suited to intimacy with an aging gay man long past his career as a sexual adventurer—if in fact he was past it. Very likely he wanted to protect me. He knew me, or thought he did, and feared I might prove faithless if I disapproved of the life he was leading.

At ninety he got a letter from a younger editor asking for permission to reprint several of his poems in an anthology of gay American poets. A fucking insult, he stormed, waving the letter at me from his white Eames chair, where he sat in offended majesty, his breathing rapid and eager. Suddenly at ninety I'm supposed to be a gay poet. Who ever told those people I was gay? I don't want an identity conferred on me. I know who I am. If the only way I can be important is to be gay then I don't want it. You wouldn't want it, would you?

I wouldn't flee from it, I said. If the shoe fits. . . .

But it doesn't fucking fit, he said, leaving me more or less speechless and exasperated. It wasn't as if other anthologists were beating a path to Irving's door asking to reprint his work. There was no principle that I could understand to account for Irving's rage and resistance.

I remembered then a night we'd spent together years before. We'd driven to a movie at a small theater in Kingston, as we often did with Irving in those days. The feature that week was Franco Brusati's *To Forget Venice*, a film that has nothing to do with Venice but a lot to do with the disappointments of a middle-aged homosexual. Irving sat between us at the theater, munching popcorn, absorbed, apparently enthusiastic, until a young man on screen came out of the bathroom, casually walked towards the camera without a stitch of clothing on, a veritable dangling man, and affectionately embraced his male lover, also undressed and visibly stirred. Wow, Irving exclaimed, so that no one in our vicinity could fail to hear him, you really get your money's worth in this one.

But throughout the remainder of the film Irving was clearly unhappy and growing grimmer by the minute. We squeezed his hands several times to signal our desire that he keep his comments to himself. In the car later he declared the film disgusting, disturbing. Disturbing how? I asked him.

Who needs, he asked, to see somebody else's sexual torment? Who would want it? There's no art in the thing. Art is concealment, isn't it, not confession. I don't mind seeing the nearness of the abyss as long as I'm not being asked to plunge headfirst into it.

But where's the abyss in this film? I asked. I don't see it. All I see is unhappy people.

A line is crossed, he said. When people inflict sexual torment on one another and I'm forced to witness it, that's pushing me over the edge. It makes me want to turn away and shut my eyes. It's ugly.

But I don't see what's so ugly, I persisted. The men have very handsome bodies, don't they?

It has nothing to do with handsome, he said. You don't see the ugliness. I can't make you see it.

We were briefly silent then, the car ploughing slowly through the freshly fallen snow as we crossed into New Paltz and saw below us the scattered town lights. I was irritated with myself for pressing my friend, and with him for seeing things as he did. I just didn't get it, I felt. Then Phyllis said something to shift the conversation a little. She leaned between us from the back seat of the car and said, So what do you think of Mapplethorpe?

Who? he asked.

You know who, she said. The photographer with all the male nudes.

That's just pornography, he said. Don't tell me you think there's anything more to that guy. You can tell why he's fa-shionable, he went on, playing out the word. He gives them what they want. A big black cock and just enough style to make them feel it's advanced.

No sexual jolt? Phyllis asked.

I've seen hard-ons before, he said.

There wasn't much on the walls of Irving's nursing home room to remind you of what he'd been. The only book in the room was his own Collected Poems. Lennie had brought him photos of Yorkies and Gilbert and Sullivan players to decorate the room. Love 'em, he said. Miss my little Yorkie like hell. Nothing I can put my hand on and get the same feeling of trust. You ever read my po-em about Yorkies?

Of course, I said. You know I've read everything you ever wrote. It's one reason, isn't it, that you dedicated the book to us?

Did I do that? he asked. I forgot. Wish I could forget the lousy food odors. Would you mind closing the door? I can smell the food an hour before they wheel in the cart. Can't touch it. Wish I could go out for a burger and fries like Lennie.

At which point Lennie sauntered in. That my name I hear you taking in vain? he asked, flopping at once into Irving's wheelchair, no smiles, no greeting.

Just saying how you like burgers, Irving said.

You got that right, old man.

See who's visiting? he asked.

Who else would there be? Lennie replied.

Could be somebody else, Irving half whispered. One or two.

Not likely, Lennie said. You ain't a lot of fun like you used to be.

I was never any fun, Irving said, not really.

Irving and his po-ems, Lennie intoned.

He's like a son to me, Irving crooned. Don't know what I'd do without him.

How's the family? I asked.

The what? Lennie asked.

Your two sons, I said. How are they?

They're alright, Lennie said. Funny question.

Is it? I said.

How's your kids? Lennie asked. See how funny it sounds? You don't know nothin' about my kids and I don't know nothin' about yours.

Never hurts to ask, does it? I asked.

Nothin' hurts you, he said. Too intel-li-gent for that.

Meaning what? I asked. Jesus, I mean all I asked is how are your kids.

Nice of you to ask, he said. Is that better?

I hated the way he talked, always familiar and derisive, hated the way he sat in Irving's chair with his legs thrust out into the room, hated the thought that over the years Irving had just maybe given him permission to dump on us, on me in particular, to mock my demeanor and my over-earnest good will. So long as the mockery would remain always their little secret and Irving might occasionally rein in Lennie's sarcasm. Though now Irving was too feeble to rein in anything.

Only once did Lennie give Irving a pain. Four or five years earlier he decided it was time to buy Lennie a little house of his own. Something modest, near Irving's place, and with a downstairs bedroom, should Irving need to move in at some point and be taken care of. We'll take care of you, Phyllis had said, but no, Irving decreed. You have a complicated life. Too many kids, too many trips.

You once said, I began, but Irving interrupted, that was before, when Lennie was an unknown quantity, and I couldn't be sure, but this will be better.

The house was a nondescript, narrow, two-story building on a quiet street, and it had the downstairs bedroom Lennie had promised to provide. We drove over to have a look the very day that Lennie moved in with his boyfriend, a tall, lanky, improbably well-spoken young man who wrote for a community newspaper. We liked him, thought he was sweet and direct. He showed us the upstairs of the place while Irving sat with Lennie in the freshly painted white kitchen making a pitcher of lemonade. We congratulated Lennie and Hank on their new house and soon drove with Irving back to his place. Yes, we approved, we said, and yes, we liked Hank, a good catch. Are they serious? Very serious, Irving assured us. I had to have the mortgage assigned to the three of us. That's the way Lennie wanted it.

Not my place to question that, I said. But did you think it was a good idea?

I said no, definitely not, Irving answered. He only knows Hank a year or so and here I'm presenting him with one-third ownership of a house. Not a great idea with gay partners. They don't stick, he said.

This one will be different, I said. Lennie's been around the block.

He falls in love, Irving said. They fall in and out of love like kids.

But that's crazy, Phyllis said.

You don't mean it, I said.

Of course I mean it, he said. My hand shook when I signed those papers.

A year later we sat with Irving in his living room, the long gauze curtains fluttering a little, the fish nosing silently through the lighted tank. Irving was sprawled on the white leather couch blowing his nose and wiping at his eyes with a red bandanna. I'd never seen him so upset, so given over to his grief.

You don't know this type, he said.

He's just a boy, Phyllis said. You make him sound like some kind of predator.

It's instinct, Irving said. He has the instinct of a predator and the good looks to disarm his prey. And the words. Lennie's no match for his smooth talk.

Lennie's a pretty sophisticated guy, Phyllis said.

The boy took advantage of him, Irving said. He saw him coming from a mile away, a perfect dupe, a mark, an easy lay. It's the sort of thing the gay ones do to each other. The nice ones fall in love and the others wrap them around their little fingers.

Since when, I interrupted, did this pattern become exclusive to gays?

Who said it has to be exclusive? Irving asked. And now, he went on, wiping again at his eyes, the little punk invites into the house another guy, a friend he calls him, with an earring, and Lennie can't help it, he has to move out, he can't sit around the house and watch Hank holding hands on the couch with his new friend.

I'm surprised Lennie didn't just order him out, or threaten him.

He's weak, Irving said, soft. He looks tough, but the punk has him exactly where he wants him.

Soon Irving hired a lawyer and got Hank to move out of Lennie's house, pocketing the cool forty thousand bucks Irving had to pay for a settlement. It's not like the old man is rich, Lennie told me on the phone one night, clearly remorseful for a change. I feel fuckin' stupid.

I know nothing about Irving's financial affairs, I said. You're the heir apparent, not me.

You're in the will, he said. Some books and pictures anyways.

I tried, harder than ever before, to like Lennie after his tribulations, but he seemed to learn nothing from his experience. He was cocky and surly and, within a week of his outburst, not the least bit remorseful about anything. He steered clear of us pretty much as he had in the past, and though we ran into one another more often at the nursing home, when Irving relied on him more than ever and Lennie was there for him every single day of the week, I was amazed at the string of boys he routinely brought along, as if Irving needed to be introduced in those final months to every single one of Lennie's conquests. What are you so uptight about? he asked me one night in the corridor outside of Irving's room. You hardly even say fuckin' hello to my friend.

When did you become so sensitive? I asked. Maybe I don't like your friend. Maybe I don't think you need to bring every stray in to visit Irv.

He approves of my taste in guys, Lennie said. He likes to see where I am.

Where you are, I repeated. Like you're going to be in the same place next week.

How do you know where I'll be next week? he asked.

I don't care where you'll be or where you are, I said, as honestly as I could. I care only about Irv's state of mind.

You don't know a fuckin' thing about his state of mind, Lennie said. You never asked him and you couldn't deal with it if he told you.

He told you that? I asked.

I know everything about you, he said. That's why I never liked you, 'cause I know you.

A lot of hostility there, I said.

You don't know how much, he said.

We looked around just then, the two of us, at the blank faces of the several inmates staring into space in their wheelchairs, lined up against the wall just down the corridor. We took in as well the two dozen smiley-face decals stuck on the wood frame around Irving's bedroom door.

Pathetic, Lennie said.

They're smiling at us, Lennie, I said. They see how hopeless we are when we try to talk with one another.

You don't fuckin' know how funny you are, he said.

When Irving died a week later Lennie took charge of the funeral arrangements, as he had been instructed to do in Irving's final testament. He called the surviving family members, nieces and nephews from Boston, an elderly sister at a rest home in Vermont, some others Irv had listed, a few former students, people Irv hadn't seen in years. It couldn't have been much of a list, I thought, and the funeral itself, we feared, would be a dispiriting, desultory affair. Would it be alright, I asked, to invite a few poets who lived nearby to read some of Irv's poems? He didn't want strangers, Lennie said. Says right on the paper he don't want no strangers doing anything at the funeral.

Understood, I said. Phyllis and I can do the reading.

Don't want that either, he said. Says right on the paper don't want it. I asked him about it and he says nobody there's gonna understand a word if you read his stuff out loud. Better just to say a few words about him and let it go.

At the funeral Lennie was dressed from head to toe in black leather, his collarless jacket buttoned up to the neck, his shiny leather boots clicking smartly on the marble floor of the funeral home parlor as he took up his station at the door, greeting everyone with a smile and a handshake, accepting condolences as if he were the one and only bereaved son of the deceased. Behind him a row of pretty young men stood at attention, all of them neatly dressed and coiffed, not one of them over thirty. Lennie's voice sounded confidently over the room, rhythmic and persistent, the prepared commonplaces rippling out one after the other. I approached the older niece from Boston, who seemed not much interested in chatting with me about Irving. It's too sad, she said, as if he hadn't made it into his nineties and had a more or less successful life. Phyllis sat and spoke with an older man who carried a cane. He looked a little like Irv, with a narrow, angular face, though of course there was a certain gaunt look you saw in the faces of the very elderly that made all of them resemble one another a bit. As I watched Phyllis talking with the man I found myself standing next to another fellow, seventy or so, very tall and with fine features and a generous head of white hair. I'm Norman, he said, leaning over me and smiling. I think I was Irv's tallest friend.

I'm sorry we never met before, I said.

Oh but I know all about you, he said. Irv spoke a lot about you. Liked the way you praised him. Kept his poetry alive, he told me. Very nice.

But how is it, I asked, that he didn't mention you to me? I don't remember him mentioning a Norman, and I bet my wife doesn't either.

I expect, he said, moving a little closer and stooping to whisper in my ear, that there are several old codgers in the room he never mentioned, not to you, at any rate, though Lennie all of us knew. He wouldn't have kept us from Lennie.

At that there was some movement in the room, and I saw that Lennie had begun to call people together for the service. The rabbi stood up at the front of the room at the side of the coffin, and I noticed that there were many more people assembled than we had anticipated. Norman had moved off to the side near the rows of folding chairs, and was greeting eight or ten older men who appeared, all of them, to know one another. They looked to be tan and fit, as if they'd spent their recent time lying out in the sun and strolling idly on a beach somewhere, the way I once imagined Irv doing at Key West. Were these, I wondered, friends he'd picked up in those days?

When the rabbi introduced the proceedings and led us in prayer, I held Phyllis's hand and looked around again at the congregation Lennie had gathered, many of them male friends of Irving, young and old, men I'd never met or heard him mention. Then I heard Lennie call my name, and I stood up and read the remarks I'd carefully composed the day before, remarks comparing Irving to the great poets he so much admired and asserting that he and his work had meant more to me and to many others than anyone else I could name. We would miss Irv himself, I said, but we had a lifetime's work to console us. The words seemed hollow to me even as I recited them, but I'd thought it was my place to say these things, to speak for that part of Irving no one else knew or loved so well. As I recited my part I looked up over the paper I held in my hand and saw that Norman was whispering something to the man who sat next to him.

When I took my seat Lennie came forward again and asked if others would care to stand and say some words about Irving—that is what he'd instructed, that those who wished to speak would speak and say what was in their hearts. The first to stand was Norman: I'm Norm Horowitz, he said, and I knew Irving over a number of years in Haiti, where I own a hotel—and then Armando Krauze: we were close to one another in Cuernavaca and never lost touch—and then nine others, not one under sixty, I thought, each speaking briefly, each having shared with Irving a past and each having remained, one way or another, in touch.

Later, at the cemetery, the proceedings completed, I stood silently, blankly, next to Phyllis. So what do you think, Lennie asked, sliding in beside me and standing close for the first time all day. I didn't know what to say. Are you listening to me? he asked. Why are you staring at my boots?

They're so . . . leathery, I said. All of you is so . . . leathery.

Listen, he said, I asked you how you liked the ceremony and all.

It was perfect, Phyllis said. Exactly the way Irv wanted it.

A few surprises in it for you, Lennie said, placing his hand on my arm.

Are you trying to provoke me? I asked.

Provoke you to what? he replied, looking directly into my eyes. I saw that his face was smooth, the skin flawless. Come on, he said, let me see you smile and say that was one hell of a beautiful funeral you pulled off, Lennie. Come on, let me hear you say it.

I gently removed his hand from my arm and said to Phyllis, we're through here. Then, stepping further away from Lennie, I looked once more at the handsome men, young and old, stooped and erect, engaged warmly in conversation, and wondered, not for the last time, why it was that at the funeral of a man I had thought so much a part of me I had felt so empty, apart, and alone. Phyllis squeezed my hand and pulled me past Lennie and away from the still chattering guests, their faces alert, their courteous animal noises lifting into the late afternoon sun.